MEMOIRS OF A TIGER

MEMOIRS OF A TIGER

AJIT MUTTU-CUMARASWAMY

iUniverse, Inc.
Bloomington

Memoirs of a Tiger

iUniverse books may be ordered through booksellers or by contacting:

iUniverse
1663 Liberty Drive
Bloomington, IN 47403
www.iuniverse.com
1-800-Authors (1-800-288-4677)

ISBN: 978-1-4759-4015-2 (sc)
ISBN: 978-1-4759-4016-9 (e)
ISBN: 978-1-4759-4017-6 (dj)

Library of Congress Control Number: 2012913775

Printed in the United States of America

iUniverse rev. date: 10/10/2012

PREFACE

Ravin sat on the nicely cushioned Colombo Airport chair and took in the scene. It was like a scene from a war film. Almost every other plane that sat on the tarmac had been damaged, its sides blown out. The coconut trees swayed gently in the background. They seemed to say, "This happens when things are done wrong."

The enemy had struck and fled – a hit-and-run attack. Nobody was guarding the wrecked aircraft. No cordons. No police cars or army trucks. Just a normal airport. Except several planes stood on the tarmac with their sides blown out.

How did people feel when they landed in Colombo Airport, called the Bandaranayake Airport and named after the man had who began a process of change that had ended up in civil war? What did passengers think when they saw blown-up planes standing on the tarmac? Did they think this part of the airport was a scrap yard? Were they aware that they were coming to a country that had been torn apart by a civil war, with the rebels in the north wanting to rule themselves?

Ravin had his tickets to London, his home for many years. He worked for a refugee charity organisation in London. The board of the charity had asked him to go and assess the situation in Sri Lanka, as more and more refugees were arriving in London from Sri Lanka. He had come to see for himself and take first-hand news to London. This was also a chance to visit friends, uncles and aunts, and cousins. Close members of his family were all in London.

His mind could comprehend the scene in front of him but could not accept it fully. He had been told that nobody had been hurt during the raid. He was staring at the scene for the second time, having seen it when he arrived from London a few days ago. He tried to make mental notes of how he would describe it to people in London.

Working for a charity, he often met persons who were members of the Liberation Tigers of Tamil Ealam (LTTE). The LTTE had been fighting to carve out a separate state for the Tamil ethnic group, which was strong in the north and east of Sri Lanka. The majority community, the Sinhalese, was vehemently opposed to separation. The LTTE had been banned in Sri Lanka and many other countries for its violent activities. Ravin's mother constantly reminded him to keep away from the group. His family had no interest in a separate state. He himself felt it was wrong to ask for separation. But he accepted that fear of reprisals by LTTE did halt attacks by thugs and politicians on Tamils living in the south. He had helped members of the LTTE to contact housing authorities when they were desperate.

He was hoping that the leader of the LTTE would soon abandon the call for a separate state. He was certain that better sense would prevail and a compromise solution would be reached soon.

He'd gained some sympathy for the LTTE only after one of his cousins had been taken away by the army and never seen again. But he had not attended any meetings or contributed money to the LTTE.

In the meantime, he was happy that some parts of the north were not under army rule. The presence of the army in the north had made matters worse. The presence of the army in Northern Ireland had led to the London bombings. This was happening in Sri Lanka now. He was happy that the aircraft were blown up while on the airport tarmac and nobody was injured.

Ravin had two hours to wait for his flight. He was glad that his flight was on a British airline. It was sad that he had this thought because he wanted to support Sri Lanka's small airline. He went to the toilet and looked at himself in the mirror. He didn't look like a harsh person, he thought. He had no stomach for causing harm. He walked back to his seat. He was tired. He closed his eyes briefly.

He sat there thinking about his life, and his thoughts took him back to his early childhood in Colombo fifty years ago.

CHAPTER ONE
KOTAHENA

R avin's family lived in Kotahena, a suburb of Colombo. Ravin often slept on the settee in the sitting room, but not when the family had visitors. He was used to visitors in the house. They were mostly relatives who came to Colombo from Jaffna. They slept on mats in the sitting room. Sometimes four or five men slept there on mats. His uncle Siva, the lawyer, came to Colombo frequently to do some of his work. He came with his wife, Danaluxmi, and two other persons. His aunt and uncle slept in the bedroom. They had three bedrooms. One was for Ravin's grandmother; one was for Ravin and his father. The third room was for Ravin's mother and two sisters.

If the visitors included a husband and wife, Mother gave her room to them. Mother came and slept in Ravin's and his father's room. This room was the largest and had a study section, with a table and chair and an ironing table in the corner. The room had two windows. One window opened onto the garden and the other into the front of the house and faced the road. The houses were built at the turn of the century but were in good condition even in the 1950s.

Standing at this window, one would see Pickerings Road and the open space leading to the road. It was a common piece of land for the five houses in the compound. Even the backyard and windows of the house next door could be seen from this window. The Cumarasamy family lived in the Colombo suburb of Kotahena.

The compound in which Ravin's house stood was called a 'garden". All the houses in the compound were owned by Mr Gomez, who was Buddhist, even though his name was Portuguese. The garden was set back from the road and had five houses and the number 85 Pickerings Road, with the five houses numbered, 85/1, 85/2, and so on. Ravin's house was the first house, and it had three bedrooms. It faced the road while the other four were terraced and faced the wall that separated the group of houses in the "garden" from the property next door. The last house in Ravin's compound had three bedrooms, but the three in the middle each had two bedrooms. All the houses had a dining room and a rear section with a kitchen, a bathroom, a toilet, and a little open cemented section. A wall separated each house from the house next door. But the open cemented section at the back of the houses had only a short wall. This was used for drying clothes and was useful for ventilation of the whole house.

The toilet was at the rear, opposite the bathroom. The chain on the water closet needed to be pulled to release the water to flush the toilet. The bathroom had a shower, a water tap, and a barrel to hold extra water. Most preferred pouring water on themselves using the water in the barrel. There was some sense in this. The shower was rarely a strong one. It only trickled water down, especially in the morning. It was never as good as a small bucket of water poured over the head in a swoosh. The water took your breath away, and you felt refreshed, especially when it was cold. The soap was on a little wooden tray mounted on the wall. There was bath soap, Lux or Rani sandalwood soap, and Sunlight washing soap for clothes.

The kitchen was bigger than in the other four houses in the terrace. By the side of the kitchen window was the fireplace. It was built on a raised brick platform. You could place three pans or pots on the fire, but the fireplace was not used very often because a kerosene cooker was now doing a lot of the cooking. Starting a fire with firewood was a problem, and firewood was not easy to get. The firewood supplier, who had his yard in Pickerings Road, moved to Santiago Street. He was also the acting physician for many households, and he was from Kerala.

The Cumaraswamy family were Tamils from Jaffna. The four other houses in the garden had Tamils from Pondicheri in India. Next to the Cumaraswamys' house lived the Pillays. Mr Pillay worked at Volkart Bros. He was fair skinned and had a very large stomach. His trousers were narrow at the bottom but blew up like a balloon when they came around his stomach. Ravin's mother blamed the big stomach on drinking a lot of toddy, a sour alcoholic drink made by fermenting coconut juice. He went to work early walking briskly and wearing a felt hat. He had two sons and a daughter. The elder was Cherubim, who was well built and had a moustache. He was in his twenties and went to work on a bicycle. The girl was going to school. And the third was a boy, Sridaran, who was Ravin's friend. He was Ravin's age, and they grew up together from the time they were toddlers. Sridaran went to St Benedict's College, while Ravin started in a school on Pickerings Road before joining St Benedict's College in grade four.

Mrs Pillay's niece and her family occupied the house next to the Pillays. They were a young couple. The next house was rented by Mr Gnanapragasam, who worked in Cargill's Department Store in the Fort as a salesman. He wore a tie to work. He had two sons and two daughters. He used to drink toddy after work and stop to talk to people for a long time. He dropped in to talk to my grandmother and mother.

He had a lisp, and the smell of toddy seemed to fill the house when he spoke.

The last house had three bedrooms and was occupied by Mr Cadelis. Mr Cadelis worked as a pharmacist. He used the third bedroom as an office and bedroom. The third bedroom opened into a small garden. Mr Cadelis was also from Pondicheri and was married to Mrs Pillay's cousin. His wife was much darker than Mrs Pillay, but she spoke to everyone with a lovely smile and children liked her. The Cadelises had grown-up children, two daughters and a son. One daughter was married, and the couple lived in the same house.

A tall, red brick wall stood at the end of the "garden".. Ravin and Sridaran used to climb the wall and sit on it. On the other side of the wall, they could see a large area that was part of the adjoining property. It was known as Bobby Arnolda's garage. Bobby Arnolda's "garage" included a large garage as well as a large house, which was set in a large garden and was the house next door to Ravin's garden. Mr Arnolda owned his large house and the garden with garages and staff houses. The garage had servicing bays, an office, covered parking bays at the back, and small houses for staff. When Ravin and Sri sat on the wall at the end of the garden, they looked into the staff houses; some had two rooms, and many had only one room.

Mr Arnolda's residence was close to the road. It had four bedrooms in a row. The front veranda could be seen from the road. Mr Arnolda's bedroom was annexed to it on the left. The door to the bedroom opened onto the veranda. The sitting room with its sumptuous furniture could be seen from the road. The bedrooms opened into the sitting room and the adjoining dining room. When they had a party,the house looked grand, with people dancing in the sitting room.

Mr Arnolda owned a taxi service that specialised in hiring cars for tourists. He had large American cars Chryslers, Plymouths, Buicks, Pontiacs, and Fords. These cars were nothing like the Ford Prefect that Ravin's uncle had. Ravin and his friends loved to admire the cars, as they were washed each morning and parked, gleaming with chromium bumper bars and the flying figure or bird on the nose of the bonnet. The drivers drove out to the Fort and parked near the jetty, facing the Grand Oriental Hotel. Some probably drove farther down to the Galle Face Green and parked near the Galle Face Hotel. They drove tourists and hotel guests around and were not for hire by locals. Mr Arnolda had smaller cars with meters for hire for local people.

Ravin's family's "garden" with the five houses was set back from the roadside. But most houses down the road had their entrances on the road. When the compound residents exited the garden and turned left down Pickerings Road, they would pass three houses whose entrances were on the road but whose backyards abutted Ravin's house. The Schockmans, who were Burghers, lived in the first one. Mr Schockman was skinny, red-faced, and had his hair parted in the middle. Mrs Schockman was fat and had a red round face and looked cross all the time. They had a son and a daughter. The son was very friendly with Ravin. He even wanted to touch Ravin's private parts. It was a nice feeling. Ravin had to do the same to him.

Next door to the Schockmans were the Fernandos, who were Sinhalese. One could see the back of their house, the toilet and bathroom, and the kitchen from Ravin's back garden. There was no fence. They had a son and two daughters. The son, Ivan, was a very friendly boy.

Ivan was somewhat younger than Ravin, but his knowledge of the world far exceeded Ravin's. He had two sisters, one of whom Ravin admired very much. Lorraine had a heart-shaped face that broke into a delightful smile whenever they met. He particularly enjoyed the dimples on her checks. She had the air of someone who had just done something naughty like stealing a spoonful of sugar. Her sister, Marie, was younger and giggled a lot.

When Ravin called on Ivan, Ravin would ask, "Is Ivan at home?"

Marie would giggle and turn pink, and her eyes would close completely as her face peeled into a smile. "He is at home," she would say, before diving out of sight into a room or behind a piece of furniture and calling out to Ivan.

If Ivan's father or mother were there, he or she would normally say, "He must be somewhere out back," and direct Ravin inside the house.

They had a boarder called Sam, a young man who was friendly but had bloodshot eyes. Ravin knew he consumed a lot of liquor. Ivan told him so. Sometimes Ivan's mother, father, and Sam would be seated at the front veranda talking. Only Ivan's father and Sam would have a drink on the floor by the sides of their chairs. But Ravin always knew when Ivan's mother had also had a drink. Her face looked flushed, and her laugher was extra loud. She was always friendly. She would inquire about Ravin's parents.

Ravin's friend, Ivan, used to embarrass him by saying that he had seen his sisters naked. He said he used to peep through the keyholes.

He invited Ravin to join him to peep at his sister having a bath. He said, "You know, I have seen my parents doing it."

Ravin would smile with embarrassment. But his curiosity was always roused.

"You should come on a Sunday afternoon," Ivan would say. "It's easy. Even my sisters are asleep. Don't worry. Nobody will catch us."

Ravin's interest in the venture must have been plain to see on his face. But the risk of being caught in the act was always too much for Ravin.

Ravin would say, "Okay, I will come around on Sunday." But when Sunday afternoon came along, he would studiously avoid going to see Ivan.

One Sunday afternoon, Ravin met Ivan as he came out of his house. "Are you headed somewhere?" Ivan asked.

Ravin remembered Ivan's offer to show him Sunday afternoon activities through the keyholes. But he couldn't think of something to say. "No," he said.

"Come. I will show you Mum and Dad doing something interesting," he said.

Ivan held Ravin by his arm and took him toward his house. They walked between the banana trees and stepped into the back veranda of his house. They walked along the dining room and stepped quietly towards the bedroom, Ivan holding him by his hand. He looked around to make sure nobody was about and tiptoed towards one of the doors, bent down, and looked through the keyhole for a while before beckoning to Ravin. Ravin stepped alongside him. Ivan stepped back and signalled to Ravin to take a look. He whispered in Ravin's ear, "I will keep a lookout. You don't worry."

Ravin peeped through the keyhole. He could only see the lower half of the bed through the keyhole. A pair of legs was stretched out. They were obviously a man's legs, large and hairy. The woman seemed to be kneeling over him. Ravin strained his eye to see the faces. His eyes were out of focus, but he could only see the pair up to the waist. He could recognise that the woman was on top. She lifted herself up quietly and lowered her body even more slowly.

A large pillow was tucked underneath. His excitement was getting too much to bear, but he could not take his eyes off the scene. On occasions, the person below had his hand underneath propping up his instrument. His friend, Ivan, came up to him and whispered in his ear, "It's all right. There is nobody about. My mum and dad stay in their room a long time."

As Ivan walked away, the couple got up from the bed. Before fleeing, Ravin could not help stealing a quick look at their faces. It was Ivan's mum and the boarder.

Ravin avoided Ivan after the incident at his house. Once, Ravin did see Ivan running out of the back of his house, creating a slashing sound as he ran in between the banana trees. His father was pursuing him with a thin short cane in his hand. But it may not have had anything to do with the incident on Sunday.

Next to the Fernandos were the Halls, who were Burghers. The Hall family were all grown up. Mother was a widow. Both sons and the daughter went to work. The older son had a Matchless motorcycle. A sheet metal fence separated Ravin's family backyard from the three others.

If one walked on Pickerings Road and turned left onto Santiago Street, passing the Cooperative Store, one passed along a block of four terraced houses occupied by the Paul family, who were Burghers and the Velayutham family, who were Tamils from Jaffna. Next door was the Maligaspe family, who were Sinhalese and Buddhists. In the last house in the row of houses lived the Smale family, who were mixed Burgher and Muslim. They were our neighbours because our backyards backed into each other.

Walking on further on Santiago Street, beyond the block of four terraced houses, there was an open area. There were shops on the roadside and small houses for workers. When Ravin walked with his friend, Sridaran, they walked up the hill, passing all the little houses. There were taps on the roadside where people bathed. Men wore their sarongs as they bathed, and women also wore sarongs. Women wore sarongs and blouses and walked barefoot sometimes.

On both sides of the road, there were little lanes, narrower than Ravin's and Sri's garden. Little lanes led to a group of houses. They knew people in one or two houses. And they would smile, and Ravin and Sri would smile back.

Sometimes they asked, "Going for a walk?"

Ravin and Sri would smile and reply, "Yes, we are walking to College Street."

One lane on the left took you to Mr Casie Chetty's house. They were Colombo Chettys. The family owned land and houses but lived very simply. Mrs Casie Chetty was very pretty, and their son, Cyril, was Ravin's age. When Ravin's grandmother visited the Chettys, Ravin would go along with her. Cyril and Ravin would go out in the garden and play.

Mr Casie Chetty was tall and slim and wore glasses. He spoke in English. Occasionally, he spoke Tamil, and it sounded very funny.

As Ravin and Sri walked further, the road sloped upwards and turned right near a group of small shops selling groceries. One could sit and drink tea and eat bread with curry in some of the shops. Along this stretch of about a hundred yards, there were houses on the right. Ravin and Sri knew some of the boys who lived along here. On the left, the parapet wall sheltered the long garden of Mr Emmanuel, a portly gentleman with a thick moustache. He was an officer in the Supreme Court. Ravin's grandmother, a Protestant, was a frequent visitor there, even though the Emmanuel family were Catholics.

Ravin's grandmother belonged to the Church of England, but her favourite church was the Methodist one. Ravin accompanied her to church and tried to sing the hymns with the rest. It was a Tamil language service.

When Ravin and Sri reached the top of Santiago Street, they were on College Street, the most desirable street in the whole of Kotahena because it was a broad road and had very nice houses, many with driveways with cars parked in them.

There was a decision to be made when they reached College Street. If they turned left, they could walk towards the harbour or return to Pickerings Road. College Street met Mutwal Road, and they could then turn left and walk along Mutwal Road until they came to Kotaboam Road on the left, a broad road. Kotaboam Street had a fork after fifty yards. The left fork was Pickerings, Road and the right fork continued as Kotaboam Street.

If they decided to go right when they reached the top of College Street, they could go a long way along Mutwal Road until they reached a forbidden spot the waters meet, where the Kelani River met the sea.

Walking along Mutwal Road, the boys saw the sea and harbour on the left but behind a strong tall sheet metal fencing. They could see nothing unless they stopped and peeped through little holes in the fencing. The view through the hole was wonderful. Ships sat inside repair yards, offices had little gardens, and then the sea stretched out before them.They always stopped to peep through the small rust holes.

Once, as the boys walked along Wall Street, Sri said, "Have you been to waters meet?"

"No," said Ravin. "I'm not allowed to go to the seaside."

"Nobody will know. Besides, we need only go near the river," Sri said.

They turned onto Mayfield Road, where some of their mutual friends stayed. Nobody was standing outside their houses, so they kept walking on, passed the Buddhist temple onto College Street.

"It's not a very long walk to waters meet," said Sri. "You don't have to go into the water. I can swim while you watch."

Ravin did not break rules easily. But it seemed like he was not actually going to the sea.

They were passing the house belonging to Mr Emmanuel.

"There is Ranjini standing," said Sri laughing and pushing Ravin towards the gate of their house playfully.

Ranjini was about their age, and Ravin had told Sri about a game he had played with her when they were younger. It was a game played with marbles. They sat on the floor spreading out their legs and rolled marbles towards each other. He had told him that she sometimes did not wear pants, and he'd lost concentration on those occasions.

Farther up the road, in one of the lanes lived his favourite girl. Her name was Maryse. She had golden brown skin and brown hair and a round face. He could not look at her without feeling as if everybody was looking at him. Fortunately, they did not know the house she lived in. If not, Sri would have tried to insist on walking past her house.

At the end of College Street, they met Mutwal Street. They turned right on this road, which led to waters meet. The sea was on the left with the harbour yards. There was a Dutch church on the landside. It was one of their favourite spots. It overlooked the harbour. They walked along the road towards waters meet. Mutwal Street swept downhill, at first, past the little huts and houses and then rose up the hill, where the houses were built above the road and had steps leading on to the road. The road went uphill and downhill until they came to waters meet. The river was on the right and the sea on the left. It was calm. The river had dark sand and dark water with things floating on it. It was hardly inviting. There were men who had come to take a dip at waters meet. It was considered a good place for Hindus to bathe, and there was a Hindu temple nearby.

Sri took off his clothes and stepped into the water in his pants. He swam inelegantly, thrashing the water.

"Come on in," he called out. "I'll teach you to swim."

Ravin was tempted. He looked around. Nobody he knew was there. He took off his clothes and waded into the water in his pants. He enjoyed the coolness of the river. The riverbed was silted. When the water was knee–deep, he stopped.

"I can't teach you to swim where you are. It's too shallow," said Sri.

Ravin moved closer until he was thigh deep in water. Sri stood about two feet away.

"Try this," said Sri and gave a demonstration of what seemed like water thrashing.

His face was inside the water. His arms and legs moved furiously, and he hardly moved. Ravin stood without any confidence in his ability to stay afloat.

"It will be easier if you move over here," said Sri, stepping up and holding Ravin's arm.

Sri stepped back to where he stood before, and Ravin moved towards him. Sri took another step into the water and disappeared from view. Ravin could feel his arm tugging at him. Sri seemed to have forgotten how to swim when he stepped back into a sudden drop in the river. Ravin felt himself being pulled down. When Ravin went down, he kicked on the muddy floor, came up, and yelled, "Help," and went down again.

Sri hardly came up because he could not kick at the floor. He clung to Ravin's arm, and Ravin went down with him again. But when Ravin kicked down and came up for air, Sri also came up.

Ravin felt his hair being pulled roughly. Somebody was dragging both of them towards the shore. When they could stand up, they saw a large dark man standing there staring at them. Ravin could only grin sheepishly to show his gratitude. The man swam away doing a breaststroke.

They put their shirts on again and started walking back. They did not say a word to their parents. They both learned a good lesson. They never went back again to the waters meet.

Ravin and Sri continued with their walks, exploring the more remote corners of Kotahena.

As Ravin and Sri came out of their garden, facing the houses was a restaurant, which was called Ruben's Tea Boutique. Ruben's sold bread, buns, and other bakery products made in the bakery on Santiago Street. Ruben's cooks made rice and curry for lunchtime. Fish curry and meat curry were on display on large trays inside glass cabinets.

Seeni sambol, a special hot, sweet and sour onion dish was always available to accompany bread and string hoppers. Men working in the harbour as labourers patronised the shop. Next to the tea boutique was the entrance to the backyards of the row of houses and shops. Sometimes Ravin and Sri walked through this to look at the backyard. Bananas trees were planted there. Children used this area to play games like marbles. There was not enough space for cricket. The garden in which Ravin and Sri stayed was enough for cricket, even though the ball often got hit onto the garage and car hire company next door. Sometimes, the ball fell onto the roof of one of the houses. This meant climbing walls and getting onto the roof. Sometimes the ball got hit hard against the window of one of the houses. The sound of broken glass immediately ended the game. All the players disappeared into their houses. There was hat collection to replace the glass. Each household had to bear the cost of replacement. A broken glass panel during the middle of the month meant a cardboard window panel for two or three weeks.

The teashop opposite Ravin's garden changed its name from Chitra Hotel to Pepper House. Cafes were normally described as hotels on the signboards. People called them tea boutiques.

When the change of name happened, the neighbours noticed that men used to come into their garden and hide hessian bags in the hibiscus bushes and in the middle of clumps of banana trees. Banana trees grew in clusters of four or five trees, and there was space in the middle for a large bag. The bag was covered with dried banana tree leaves, which normally hung down by the side of the tree.

Ravin's family and the neighbours found out that the bags contained bottles of toddy, the white sour alcoholic drink that looked like milk. Made from coconut juice, toddy was stronger than beer. The bags were hidden in the bushes because of the likelihood of police raids. The strong fermented smells prevented the neighbourhood boys from drinking the liquid.

The neighbourhood boys also noticed that men working in the cafe started coming to the rubbish heap and dustbin at the top of the garden. The men would stash a packet at the bottom of the heap and later remove it. This stashing and removing of the packets took place intermittently throughout the day. It was known to all the residents that the packets contained ganja, another word for cannabis.

One day, Ravin and Sri were standing at the top of their garden. They were observing the activities on the road. Ruben Singho's younger son came up to them and asked, "What are you looking at?"

Not realising what was on Ruben's son's mind, Ravin answered, "We are not looking at anything special."

Ruben Singho's son was expecting a more apologetic answer. Ravin's answer was defiant. "Don't give me any trouble, okay," he said and pushed Ravin hard.

Ravin stumbled and fell. When Ravin picked himself up, Ruben Singho's son was standing against Ravin menacingly. Ravin's arm shot out and connected with the son's mouth. The boy looked shocked, and blood dripped from his lips. Ravin and Sri took to their heels and hid in their respective houses. About five minutes later, Ravin came to a window and looked out. He saw the boy's father, Ruben Singho, striding towards their house. Some of his men stood at the top of the lane, and one of them held a lit torch of cloth soaked in oil and tied to a stick. The flame seemed to be burning faintly due to the sun.

Ruben Singho thumped loudly on Ravin's door. Ravin's mother went to the door. Ruben Singho held his sarong menacingly high. He asked for Ravin's father. When Ravin's father came to the door, he pointed towards the top of the lane and threatened to burn the house down. Ravin's father asked why he was doing this. Before he could explain, Ravin hid himself behind a bookshelf. Ravin learned later that Ruben

Singho delivered a severe warning and went away. The following year, Ravin heard reports that Ruben Singho set fire to shops owned by Tamils. He believed all the reports.

Ravin and Sri stayed at home after school for many weeks after that incident.

After many weeks, sometimes, they would walk up Pickerings Road, which was up a hill. After passing the turn left to Santiago Street, the first house on the left was Mr Duraiswamy's. Next to the house was the family workshop, an open one where men produced silver and brass handmade pots and vases and sometimes statues of Hindu Gods. Next was a house with four families, one family to one room. The Suppiah family and the Arumugam family were Ravin's family friends. Ravin's grandmother knew them from the days when Ravin's grandfather was a tea maker in Nawalapitiya, up in the hill country in the middle of Sri Lanka.

On the right-hand side, a hair dressing salon sat opposite Santiago Street. Next door was the entrance to a large building set in a large garden. If one entered the garden, one got the feeling that this was a small town or village. In fact, it was a very large two-storey house, with a large staircase in the middle, about a dozen rooms upstairs, and almost as many downstairs. Many people lived in the building, mostly renting single rooms. It must have been a large family house, now rented out as rooms.

Various cars and rickshaws were parked there. The rickshaw pullers rented rooms in the building or slept on the veranda. The tailor who made Ravin's shorts lived here. Sometimes Ravin would be asked to go and get a rickshaw for his mother or father or grandmother. The rickshaw was handy to go to the doctor or even to neighbouring roads or to go to the bus stand or to the Kotahena market. Often a rickshaw puller would call out while Ravin's mother or father walked. Maybe he could sense a tiredness in the way they walked.

"Where are you going, madam?" the rickshaw puller would say. "Get in please. I will take you there."

At this point, if money was short, it would be polite to say, "Sorry. I want to walk."

If enough money was available, then the answer would be, "All right, but make it fast. We don't want to be late."

Rickshaw pullers came in only one shape – skinny. They were all Indians and almost all looked like they were likely to exhaust themselves if they moved fast. But they usually picked up speed quickly. They could go through tiny gaps and small lanes, taking all the shortcuts. The bell fixed onto the long handle of the rickshaw's harness was like a bicycle bell. It rang out fairly often because the roads were narrow and without pavement. People walked on the road. There was no pavement except on the main road. Sometimes, bullock carts loaded with coconuts or bags of rice or flour slowed down the flow of traffic.

Plenty of bicycles squeezed in and out of the traffic. Some young cyclists hung onto lorries with one hand to speed them along to their destinations. It was illegal and the cyclists had to look out for the police. Often, cyclists even hung on to bullock carts to rest their legs briefly and to cool off before pedalling again.

Passing the large house with lots of people living there, there was a tea boutique that made vegetarian food – pancakes from black lentils and rice flour served with soup made of red lentils, pumpkin, aubergines, and onion, along with coconut sambol. They also served savoury doughnuts made from urud dhal called vadai and steamed rice cakes shaped like little buns.

After the tea boutique on the right was the entrance to another "garden". There were six or seven houses here, some built recently. Ravin's friend, Ahmadeen, lived here.

On the left-hand side of Pickerings Road, after the Suppiahs, lived the Chandrawarnams, Ravin's grandmother's favourite family and chat group. They owned the bakery on Santiago Street. Through a clever layout, one could go through their house and walk into the bakery, which had its entrance on Santiago Street.

Next to the Chanrawarnam's was the grandest house on the whole road. It had a driveway of about a hundred metres leading to the beautiful house with a veranda all around the house. Mr Gomez, the owner, owned many houses, including the house Ravin lived in. One could walk along Mr. Gomez's driveway, pass his beautiful house, and continue and turn right, and after a few minutes of walking, join Kotahena Street. After passing Mr Gomez's house, smaller houses with large gardens could be seen. But they were quiet places. No traffic passed through. Nobody had cars or motorcycles.

On Ravin's road, Pickerings Road, Mr Gomez owned one of the few cars. The Arnoldas owned many cars, mostly for hire.

Opposite Mr Gomez's house were three houses with frontage on the road. One was a postmaster whose family regularly invited Ravin's grandmother and mother to step in and have a chat.

Next on the right was another "garden," named Esakimuttu Place. This had rows of houses on the left and right, maybe ten on each side.

Ravin's grandmother and Ravin (sometimes his mother joined them) visited the Vanderkoon family, who were Tamils from Batticaloa. They lived on the left row in Esakimuttu Place.

Lucy Vanderkoon was an attractive woman with fair skin and a beautiful smile. She always served tea or soft drinks; sometimes with biscuits.

Opposite Esakimuttu Place, the houses had frontage on the road, except for the house owned by another Arnolda, which had a large gate and the house was set inside it. The main point of interest was that this Arnolda wore a military uniform and had a stunning wife. She looked like an actress from Hollywood. Sri and Ravin always hoped to see her on their walk. Their two daughters were presentable but looked more like the father.

On the right next to Esakimuttu Place was this house with a street frontage, and after that came the Uppukulam School, which means "Salt Lake School". It was a primary school. But being a building about thirty metres long, it could only accommodate five classes.

The "garden", in which the school was set, also led to a garage that had four or five cars. The second Arnolda owned these cars. These cars also went to Fort and parked near hotels to transport tourist and visitors.

You could see the oxygen factory of the Ceylon Oxygen Company on the other side of the fence. The entrance to the company was on Kotaboam Road.

On the left side of Pickerings Road facing the Uppukulam School was a nice house. The owner seemed a rich man but did not own a car. He wore a tropical hat and a beige cotton suit on his way to work. Next on the right were two houses with a road frontage. A house with a long drive way was next. Ravin's grandmother and mother visited them occasionally. The ladies from these houses visited Ravin's family too.

Next to Uppukulam School were two houses. The Fernandopulles moved into one of them. Later on, Ravin became friendly with the five boys in the family.

Next on the right hand side of the road was a garden that led to a firewood depot. Logs were brought there for chopping into firewood. Handcarts with metal rims transported firewood to houses on Pickerings Road and other roads.

After passing the firewood depot, Pickerings Road climbed steeply. Rickshaw pullers slowed down here. Walking up, one passed three smaller houses with road frontage. Ravin's mother and father had lived in one of these when they'd first gotten married. The present occupier rode a bicycle to work. He always greeted Ravin's family when they passed along.

On the left of the road were the Leonards. Mr Leonard always came out and spoke to Ravin's mother. Mr Leonard's daughter worked in the cigarette factory. They were of Portuguese and Sinhalese origins.

As one walked farther up Pickerings Road towards Kotahena Street, there were shops along the right and one shop on the left called Peter's Store. Peter's Store was on the corner, facing Kotahena Street. Peter's Store had items that other shops did not have butter, bacon, cheese, and other goods that needed to be kept cool – because it was the only store with a refrigerator.

Ravin and Sri often walked up Pickerings Road and turned right into Kotahena Street, where the road sloped down towards the Kotahena roundabout. On the right was Mariamman Temple, followed by houses on both sides set high above street level. On the left was a vegetarian restaurant followed by houses. One could only see the steps of the houses at street level because they were set high. It was as if the road was cut deep into the hill to drain water.

Walking downhill on Kotahena Street, the boys reached the crossroad called Bonjean Road. At the junction of Bonjean Road and Kotahena Street were a shop selling ice cream and a photo studio.

Looking left, one could see St Lucia's Cathedral. By the side of the cathedral was St. Benedict's College, which was built around a sports' green. This was their school. Ravin and Sri usually headed for the church. They would sit on the ledges or the curving steps or the staircases outside the church and enjoy the peaceful scene. St Lucia's Cathedral was built on a platform with steps to go up. It had magnificent huge pillars outside and a huge dome set very high. Statues of saints stood against each pillar inside the church.

Sitting on the steps of the church, one could see the Good Shepherd Nunnery and convent school up above. Ravin's mother taught at the convent school. The steps leading up to the building were done so attractively that Ravin and Sri enjoyed walking up the steps and looking into the hall of the nunnery. The walls had air vents in the shape of a vase with flowers in it, and the hall looked calm and peaceful with several polished chairs for visitors.

Sometimes, the boys could hear a piano being played, and they would stop a while to listen. Looking beyond, through the hallway of the nunnery, they could see the grounds of the Good Shepherd Convent. The convent had its entrance on the opposite side, on Wasala Road. It occupied a large space like St Benedict's College, going from Kotahena Street to Mayfiend Road and Wall Street.

Often, they would slide down the drain alongside the steps leading to the nunnery. Sometimes, they would sit on the ledge built alongside the nunnery building. It was a vantage point from which they could see the roofs of the houses in Wall Street.

By the side of the ledge was a little hall about the size of a large classroom. This little hall became a cinema on Saturday mornings at 10:00 a.m. Father Martin, who was a Frenchman, had his little film show for children. The children paid ten cents the price of a bus fare for a short ride. He showed 16 mm films, and the projector was placed at the back of the room. He showed Charlie Chaplin films and The Three Stooges shorts regularly. Sri and Ravin rarely missed out.

Walking down the steps of the Cathedral, going along Wall Street, a lane led to Bloemendhal Road. This road led to Mutwal at one end and the junction of Grandpass Road and Armour Street at the other end. They found the road very quiet, almost like countryside.

They rarely walked down Bloemendhal Road. This changed after they started riding bicycles. Being a quiet road, this became a favourite road for riding the bicycle all the way to Mutwal.

Ravin and Sri sometimes walked up their road, and on reaching Kotahena Street, they would turn left. Peter's Store, with its exotic food and chocolates, always held a fascination. After Peter's Store and a few other smaller stores was Dharbar Hotel. It specialised in Muslim-style cooking. The Dharbar sold roti, a thin crispy pancake, and dhal curry or meat curry. The roti was rolled into rolls with meat and potato or fish and potato stuffed inside. The hotel also served Muslim sweets in various colours and sherbets in various colours with kasa kasa, little seeds, floating, along with pieces of ice.

Opposite Dharbar Hotel was Cathedral College, a small school whose principal was Mr Welcome, an Indian gentleman from Kerala. This school was for older children. Wasala Road was next to Cathedral College. This road led to the Good Shepherd Convent gate.

Sometimes, the boys walked back from the Kotahena roundabout, walking uphill along Kotahena Street and past Pickerings Road. The parade of shops on Kotahena Street continued on both sides. On the left, after Dharbar Hotel, were some shops and a few houses and then the Lord Ganesha Hindu temple set above street level. Ravin's mother often took Ravin and his two sisters to this temple on a Friday evening. They took coconut and bananas to the temple. On the way to the temple, they would be walking with Buddhists going to the Buddhist temple, dressed in white and carrying flowers in baskets.

Sometimes, Ravin's mother and father and sisters would visit the Buddhist temple carrying flowers, especially on Buddhist festival days like Vesak. This was always exciting because the Buddhist statue was very big and long – a reclining Buddha. It gleamed in the oil lit place of worship. The flames from the lamps made the statues come alive as if a gentle giant was lying down and smiling a welcoming smile and inviting the visitors to sit and take some time to make contact with their spiritual beings.

They would place the flowers they bought alongside the statue and sit down and close their eyes for a few minutes.

A few Muslims lived down Pickerings Road. One had a small shop, which was at the entrance to the house. This shop sold a variety of items of food. Some were berries rarely seen in other shops. Sweet steamed jelly-like items were Ravin's favourite. They were served in small pieces of banana leaves along with coconut. The shop also sold sweet hoppers, which looked like crumpets with a thin crusty surrounding.

The men wore fez, bell-shaped red hats with a tuft of black silky strings at the top. The silky strings fell down the hat and shook as they walked. The women covered their hair with their saris. The closest mosque was about a mile away. But sometimes the call to prayer could be heard at Ravin's house.

Ravin's inquisitiveness was roused when Muslims had funerals. Muslims did not use coffins. They carried the body on a board or wicker tray; the body was wrapped in a cotton cloth. The procession of mourners carrying the body sang out prayers while they walked quickly. All the kids ran out to the roadside to witness the procession. But there were no bands playing as in Christian funerals. During Christian funerals, drums and trumpets led the way. And the steps were measured, in a slow march towards the cemetery. And all wore black clothing. Buddhist and Hindu funerals had no drums or instruments playing. And all wore white clothing, as with Muslim funerals.

One Sunday, Ravin heard the beating of drums. A lot of activities were going on at the harbour end of Pickerings Road. This particular drum sound was only heard on rare occasions such as weddings.

At that end of the road, the harbour end, there were two small grocery shops and several groups of smallish houses set back from the street. Most of the men living in these houses worked in the harbour or the cigarette factory located on Mutwal Street.

Ravin took a walk to the end of street to find out the reason for the activity. It was a wedding or some kind of celebration. On such an occasion, five or six women sat around a large drum about two metres in diameter, called a rabana, placed on the ground. The sound of the rabana being beaten could be heard far away. It was a cheerful beat, and it indicated some kind of celebration. Ravin's friend, Ivor, joined him.

Many of the harbour workers were labourers without family and spent a lot of money on alcohol, especially toddy and arrack made from coconut juice. They left their shirts unbuttoned except for the last button at the bottom of the shirt.

Ravin never completely understood the reason for their leaving the shirts open, but he thought it was to show off their strong chest muscles. The shirt hung over the sarong, which was tucked tight around the waist but left to hang loose below the waist. They also had a handkerchief tied around their necks. The handkerchief could even be tied around the head covering the forehead and knotted over the ears in the fashion of pirates.

A broad belt around the waist with a large buckle was a must. It was not so much to hold the sarong firm as to produce an image, a suggestion of dash, verve. The belt had a pocket for money, and keys dangled from the belt for effect. A wristwatch was a sign of affluence.

Having at least one tooth filled with gold was a sign of someone who had sampled luxuries.

Even the mention of a fight set up expectations in Ravin. Fights frequently broke out in the street, but it was more a ritual than actual blows being exchanged. The two men would stare at each other with their sarongs raised to waist level and say things like, "Come on if you want to fight," in Sinhalese.

"Who wants to fight with a weakling like you?" would be the reply.

At this stage, the spectators would keep their expectations under cover and say, "Why do you want to fight over nothing?" or something to that effect.

The women fought more often. Ravin, his friends, and all spectators treasured these occasions. If any one of Ravin's friends heard of a fight brewing, he would rush and call the others. They would drop everything, even carelessly leave the cricket bats or footballs, and rush to the scene of action. Raised voices and interested people rushing in the same direction would guide the boys to the place where the action was.

The fights would begin with the women abusing each other with the Sinhalese equivalents of four-letter words.

"You prostitute" one woman would yell.

"You sperm" the other would reply.

This would be followed by a string of insults and words referring to the lower parts of a woman's body. These words were especially abusive when spoken in Sinhalese.

Often it led to one of the women raising her sarong. This was a very vicious insult – a flash of the inner sanctum, fleeting though it was. Ravin and the boys held their breath so as not to miss even a fraction of a second of the exposure.

The counter to such an insult was to rush forward and grab the opponent's hair. The two women would then pull at each other's clothes for a firm grip, slap each other, and push each other to the floor. At this point, the spectators would separate them, as if to say, "Now that you have vented your anger, you should be going home."

Ravin and others would smile at each other gleefully and say, "Did you see?" Such a fight provided a topic of discussion for several days.

The women, many of whom sold fish they'd bought at the market along the street, fought more often.

Ravin's family went to the feast of St Mary each year, even though they were Hindus. The main attraction was the procession. The procession passed New Chetty Street. The family stood on the steps of a friend's house and watched the procession. The statue of St Mary was carried at the middle of the procession. The street was decorated overhead with bunting and shiny stars, saints, and angels. At intervals of about a hundred yards, a lotus flower was suspended overhead. It was in a closed position. When the statue of St Mary passed below the lotus flower, it opened and showered glittering stars and confetti on the statue.

During the Buddhist Vesak festival, which celebrated the attaining of nirvana a state of bliss by Lord Buddha, Ravin's family went on long walks to see the various pandals (large billboards) erected in various parts of Kotahena and Grandpass. Each company or shop built a pandal with bamboo scaffolding. Artists painted the Buddha, mostly sitting up or lying down sideways. Incidents from his life were also depicted on the paintings, such as Gautama the Prince leaving the royal palace and becoming a monk. In the night, the pictures were lit up with coloured electric lights, which moved in circles. Generators roared away, producing electricity for the display. Free lemon drinks and tea and coffee were offered to sightseers. Even food was offered in some places.

Temple dancers sometimes performed in groups. They wore headgear like turbans and white pantaloons. The dancers were accompanied by drummers and musicians who played an instrument that looked like a clarinet. They started off from a convenient place, such as a Buddhist temple, and danced on the street accompanied by drums and flutes until they returned to the temple. People gathered on both sides of the street to watch the procession. Cars and vehicles had to find another route or wait until the procession had passed.

Many people came out from their homes to watch the Hindu "Theyrr" carriage on certain days. On this day, the statue of the deity in the temple was moved out of the temple and placed on a wooden carriage called "Theyrr". It was a tall structure with many wood carvings depicting gods and goddesses from the Hindu pantheon. The statue was placed in the middle of the carriage with garlands of flowers. The priest sat on the side, performing rituals with camphor, flowers, water, and ghee. The bullocks pulling the carriage were decorated with garlands around their heads, and their horns were decorated with tiny garlands. The bullocks seemed to have entered the spirit of the occasion because they stood calm and placid while there was loud drumming and music from the clarinet-like instrument called nadaswaram. The drums and the nadaswarams produced a dramatic effect. Even persons who were not Hindus held their hands together and prayed. Holy ash was distributed in brass trays with sandalwood paste and red kumkum powder. Even non-Hindus touched the holy ash and rubbed it on their foreheads, followed by a finger dip in the sandalwood paste, which was also applied on the forehead. The red kumkum powder was applied last on top of the sandalwood paste on the forehead.

Devotees offered coconuts, flowers and bananas on trays. Trays were returned with holy ash and half a coconut and some flowers and leaves used in the puja.

While attending St Benedict's College, Ravin made lots of new friends. All his friends lived within walking distance of the college. He was invited to their houses after school, and he came to know many new families living within shouting distance of the college and St Lucia's Cathedral.

He also walked with his new friends to new places and lanes not far from the college. His friends introduced him to their parents, many of whom knew about Ravin's parents, as his mother was teaching at Good Shepherd Convent, which adjoined St Benedict's College.

At the end of the year, Ravin's performance was assessed as poor, and it was all put down to his roaming around Kotahena with his schoolmates. Ravin's mother and father took him to St Joseph's College, and he got admitted there. Ravin's performance improved dramatically, and he topped his class in the first term examinations, vindicating his mother's view that he would never make good at St Benedict's College.

Ravin made lots of new friends. Most arrived in plush cars, cars like Pontiacs, Chryslers, and Plymouths. He found his new classmates all very friendly, and soon he lost concentration in class. But he did well enough to progress to the next grade each year.

One Sunday, visitors from Jaffna arrived, and Ravin's mother had to do extra cooking. Uncle Thillairaja had come for a short training course for school principals. Ravin's father and mother and uncle were talking about schools with Ravin's father and mother.

Ravin's Mother was preparing dinner. Some dishes were already on the table.

"We are teaching in Tamil in Jaffna, but when it comes to university entrance, our books are not good enough," said Uncle Thillairaja.

"At university, the students find it difficult to cope with the work. That's what I heard," said Ravin's father.

"They should never have changed to Sinhalese and Tamil," said Ravin's mother.

"In India, it's much better I'm told. The government is not interfering in the affairs of the universities. They leave it to the academics to decide. The professors stick to English for most subjects. Certainly, science is taught in English from secondary school," said Uncle Thillairaja.

"When they tried to make Hindi the official language, the South Indians rebelled and refused to comply. Thanks to that,

English is still used in schools, and Indian graduates can find jobs anywhere in the world," said his father.

"Our young boys are in a difficult situation," added Uncle Thillairaja. "They are good students, but they know that, whether they work hard or not, they will struggle to find jobs. The rumour is that the government is going to impose a quota for Tamil students entering university. Jaffna students are feeling lost. Soon we will have problems because their energies are being focussed on solving the big problem generating jobs in the north and east now that the no jobs are available for them in the south."

"We are also having rebels who see the Sinhalese as the oppressors," replied his father. "They want to break away from domination by the Sinhalese. They want complete separation. But this won't be easy."

"I am opposed to this idea," said his mother. "We must be one country. We are too small to be separated. And besides, I for one would not want to be living in Jaffna. I love Jaffna, but to think that I need a visa to come to Colombo is horrible. And I love the hill country. It is too much to think that I could not move around this little island without visas and such nonsense."

UncleThillairaja nodded his agreement. He sipped his tea and shook his head exasperation.

"Our Jaffna people are very difficult to get on with too. We are much better off staying as one country, but we need our little space. The federal solution is the best. Unfortunately, the Buddhist priests have set their faces against this. I don't understand this at all," said Uncle Thillairaja.

Ravin's father sighed deeply and looked out the window before replying"I agree with you," firmly.

"Ordinary grass-roots people are not intolerant. They understand that something harmless like a federal solution will satisfy the Tamils. Our main obstacle to a federal solution is the yellow menace. These yellow robed Buddhist priests have too much say in this country. They might even enter Parliament, which would be against everything Lord Buddha preached."

Ravin's father's legs moved in and out rapidly as the conversation was thought provoking.

Uncle Thillairaja said: "I am told that, even in Thailand, they have the same problem. Buddhist monks are leading a double life. They dress in a robe and go out pretending to be good religious people. In fact, they have women and even children. Some have even Mercedes Benz cars. Being a Buddhist priest is a profession for them. They can lay their hands on money collected at the temples. There is no law to keep their hands clean."

Ravin's father clasped his hands and stretched themup before resting the palms of his hands against the back of his head.

"It was a big mistake to make Sinhalese the state language. Both Sinhalese and Tamil should have been made state languages, like in Singapore," said Father.

"But that was the clever scheme by Mr Bandaranayake to come to power. He promised the forbidden fruit," said Uncle Thillairaja.

"It was a bitter fruit," Father replied. "It has spawned the bad feeling between Sinhalese and Tamils. Mind you, Muslims are Tamil speakers too. They are not too upset, but they must feel annoyed too."

"English could have been included, as in Singapore, to make Burghers feel all right," said Mother.

"Bandaranayake knew he would cause a feeling of deprivation. But he was going to make a federation and make Tamil the language of the north and east," said Uncle Thillairaja.

"I agree," said Mother. "Sadly, he did not allow for the strong anti-Tamil feeling among the Buddhist priests and some opportunist Buddhists."

"Many countries have been ruined by such sudden and foolish changes. In fact, the Colebrook Reforms must be blamed for the problems between Tamils and Sinhalese," said Ravin's father.

"Are you talking about the single administration for the whole country?" asked Uncle Thillairaja.

"Exactly. I'm sure that you know that during the Portuguese and Dutch rule, the north and east were governed by a different set of laws and had a different administration. In fact, when the British governor was told to unify the two administrations, he said it was impossible," said Father

"Yes," said Uncle Thillairaja. "I remember that. If only they had listened to the governor, we wouldn't be facing this problem today, the majority riding roughshod over the minorities. Sinhala Buddhist chauvinism is going to ruin the country."

"Legislation was passed in the British Parliament unifying the two administrations. All the powers became vested in the majority race. I'm not sure this was intentional, to divide and rule. When you look at the history, you can't blame the Sinhalese for using the powers. I hope we have a good leader who will make amends with a federal constitution," said Father.

Dinner was served and Ravin's mother's omelettes with onions and green chillies were commented on favourably. Her cooking was limited to the omelette and sothi, a tomato, green chilli, and onion soup cooked in coconut and eaten with a spoonful of rice as the last bit of the meal. The rest of the cooking was done by Punyawathy, Ravin's mother's adopted sister.

They finished their meal and adjourned to the front of the house.

CHAPTER TWO
JAFFNA

R avin's family looked forward to visiting Jaffna for holidays. Ravin particularly wanted to ride on the horse cart from Jaffna Station to the house in Navalar Road, which had the name board "Ward & Davy" on the front wall and "Navalar Kottam" on the door frame. Ward & Davy was the business name of the firm that Ravin's grandfather ran. Navalar Kottam was the name of the residence. Navalar was the name of a scholar who translated the Bible into Tamil but later rebelled against the colonial system and wanted to maintain the old Hindu traditions.

The school holidays usually meant that all of Ravin's family members were on holidays, since both his parents were teachers. Preparation for departure included packing suitcases and canvas holdalls. Ravin's father packed books and manuscripts in cardboard boxes. These boxes caused tension because Ravin's mother was against carrying additional luggage. They caused tension even in Jaffna because Ravin's grandfather scolded Ravin's father for trying to publish his books without having money for the paper. Sometimes, Ravin's father wrote books that were put on the government-approved list of schoolbooks to be purchased by students.

Two days before the departure, Ravin's family would go to the Hindu temple in Kochikade with rice, coconuts, flowers, and bananas. After going to the temple and praying, they would go to the houses set back from the temple meant for the priests. Sometimes they sat there until one of the priests or assistants, who were all Brahmins, came to talk to Ravin's family. Ravin's mother would ask for the rice to be cooked in a special way and hand over the rice and some money. They would go back the next day to collect the cooked rice before going to the station to catch the train. It was a special rice with yoghurt and spices, which was wrapped in banana leaves and then in newspaper and placed in a brown paper bag. Everything, except for vegetables, was placed in brown paper bags, even in shops. But the bags had no handles. Everyone took clothe bag or bags made with sisal or hemp to fetch things from shops.

The family trip commenced with a taxi ride in a Morris Minor. Ravin's grandmother would stay back with ravin's mother's adopted sister. Punyawathy did mostly housework but had authority over the children and accompanied the family to the cinema and fundraising school carnivals.

The taxi took the family to Fort Railway Station. They queued up for tickets. Sometimes, Ravin's father had purchased the tickets the previous day. The gatekeeper clipped the the tickets as they went through the gate. And the gatekeeper knew which platform they should go to. The Jaffna night train was given platform number one each night, since it was always full and earning the best money for the railway.

Finding a good carriage, called a compartment was always a problem. So the family would always rush on board. Sometimes they were lucky and got window seats facing each other. Mother would sit at one window, and Ravin would sit opposite. Ravin's mother always called his father "I say". "I say, please sit next to Ravin," she would say. Ravin's father would not hesitate to carry out the request.

Sometimes, last-minute arrivals would push their bags through our window, requesting politely that we place the bag on a seat until they could fight their way in. Close to the time the train was supposed to leave, a crowd usually rushed in, and the doors would be jammed with people trying to board the train. This could have been at weekends. Many Jaffna men worked in Colombo and went to Jaffna for the weekends.

The whistle blew at the time of departure. A guard would walk from the locomotive end of the train to the tail end, where the guard's van was stationed. The stationmaster or another official would come out of his office and wave the green flag. The locomotive would let off a whistle with its steam, followed by a lunge forward as the brakes were released. But the train was still boardable. People who had rushed outside to buy food would be boarding at that moment. Doors would open and people would get in as the train moved. Ravin enjoyed watching the last-minute people. The train was moving but very slowly. Doors opened to let men into the train even as the carriages were leaving the platforms.

Only when the last carriage had passed the platform would the locomotive let off a huge horn-like sound and you could hear the steam being let off and the chug chug noise became clear. The burning coal smell would start drifting down, which would make Ravin happy. He enjoyed the smell, and so did his family. He would even feel a pang of hunger and excitement at the thought of the food parcels being opened shortly, especially the food parcel prepared by the priest at the Siva temple in Kochikade.

Nobody opened food parcels until a few stations, like Gampaha, had passed. Until then, passengers could see and enjoy the lights of the big town of Colombo as the train sped away and the movement of the train became a sort of waltz. Some people were already falling asleep and opening their mouths as they slept in a seated position. Some were leaning on their neighbours. Since it fell to Ravin's father to sit next to strangers, he would be the person taking the brunt of such leanings and shoulder restings.

Very few brought books. Ravin's father would try to read in the poor light. Even before the train took off, moths and bugs would buzz around the half globe, and strangely, Ravin could see some dead bugs inside the glass globe casing. This made Ravin wonder how they got inside the glass casing, and his eyes searched carefully around the light for a little nook through which the insect could have gotten through.

Ravin and his sisters, Bhanu and Shamba, eagerly awaited the food parcels. Ravin's father sometimes rushed out of the station and bought a food parcel of lentil pancakes and red lentil soup and coconut sambal. It could be two parcels one with lentil pancakes and the other with rice cakes. But it was the yoghurt rice made by the priest at Siva temple that was the irresistible parcel.

Ravin's mother would open the parcel of yoghurt rice and wash her hand with the bottle of water, which she held outside the window. The others also would wash their hands. Sometimes, she would give out pieces of banana leaf to each of them to place on their palms. She would make spicy yogurt rice balls and place them on the banana leaf, and Ravin and his sisters and father would enjoy the delicious food. The combination of spices, ghee, and yoghurt was a firm favourite. The banana leaf and newspaper wrapping would go out of the window, neatly wrapped and tied with the sisal string.

A second parcel would open, and the contents would be eaten in portions divided up by Mother. The passengers would ignore the activity, or some would open their own food parcels. Some would try to sleep.

After the dinner, they would use of the bottles of water held outside the window to wash their hands. They drank water to wash it all down. Sometimes, a flask of tea or coffee was consumed to finish off the meal.

Conversations were sometimes opened up with fellow passengers, and usually they were about family connections and doings. Lots of names of relatives and friends were mentioned until one was familiar. The connections were then unravelled based on this person. Mention was made of his or her present whereabouts, what job he or she was doing or school he or she attended, and where his or her family resided. Ravin's father would mention his father's name and the name of the press he was running, and most people knew about it. The passenger would ask questions about his father's brothers. Ravin's father had five brothers and four sisters.

His father and the passenger would take some time to discuss their connections. At this point, Ravin would sometimes feel sleepy. If they were on the right side of the carriage, which had no doors, he would be lucky. He could sleep on the floor of the carriage. A newspaper or a piece of cloth would be spread on the floor, and he would sleep mostof the way.

If he woke up halfway through the journey, it would be because of some unusual jerk. The train could have come to a halt because of signal failure. Sometimes it was because the train had reached a station like Madawachiya or Maho.

Arriving at one of the stations signalled a host of activities sufficient to wake people up. If Ravin woke up, he could hear vendors saying, "Tea, tea, tea, tea," and others saying, "kopee, kopee, kopee, kopee." If he stood up and looked out he could see men with trays of tea and coffee with sugar and milk added. The tea or coffee would be in small drinking glasses.

Other vendors also walked the platform. Some called out, "bunnis, bunnis, bunnis." These were baked buns made from wheat flour that were soft and sweet.

Customers would lean out of windows, handing out money and receiving tea or coffee and coins as change. Others would have stepped out of the train, stretched themselves, and decided to have tea or coffee.

If the train had passed Anuradhapura and reached northern areas, there would be other vendors saying, "vadai, vadai, vadai." Vadai were lentil balls made with split lentils soaked in water and then formed into little balls with onion and chilli and fried. This was a popular item.

Vendors walking around the platform also sold cigarettes and "beedies". Beedies were made from a small special aromatic leaf rolled into a tiny cigarette. They were much cheaper than cigarettes. Instead of carrying matches to light cigarettes, the vendors had a sort of rope made of light sisal hanging down from the tray. This rope burned slowly from the end that was hanging down. Anyone needing to light a cigarette, beedie, or cigar had only to stop the vendor and light his cigarette or other smoke by lifting the rope up to his smoke. Women never smoked in public. When the smoke was lit, the rope was dropped to hang out of the tray, glow, and let out smoke of its own.

The hot drinks were complemented by bottles of cold drinks. Vendors called out, "Lanka Lime" three times or "Orange Barley" three times. Very rarely did they call out "Cream Soda," which was the other popular bottled aerated water drink. The price of a bottled drink was about three or four times more than tea or coffee, and there were fewer customers for the bottled aerated waters.

Looking out of the train window at Maho or Madawachiya, Ravin could not see much. Lots of fireflies flew about with sparks and the light from the locomotive sometimes shone out onto the track. Sometimes the engine needed water as it was a steam engine. He could see water chute being connected to the locomotive. The smell of burning coal drifted about pleasantly.

The train would ease itself out of the station without much of a hoot in deference to the sleeping passengers. Once the train resumed its rhythm, the gentle swaying from side to side would be sufficient to induce another bout of sleep on the floor. Ravin's sisters were rarely asked to sleep on the floor, possibly because their skirts could sometimes lift up. Ravin would sometimes look forward to such exposure to satisfy his curiosity about such parts of the female anatomy. In the house, he had occasionally feasted his eyes on such hidden parts.

The train ride was very special on moonlit nights. The shadow of the train moving took on a special rhythm and movement.

As the train glided along, the trees and the landscape took on a fascinating glow. The forests were like gardens in the moonlight. The branches of the trees seemed to be gently swaying and moving to the rhythm of the train. Occasionally, the moon could be seen. Ravin used to look intently into the forest, wondering whether he could see an animal or a person. He never did see an animal or a person in the night.

The train would move fast until Anuradapura. This stretch had a special effect on Ravin. Instead of going from side to side, the train seemed to be going up and down gently. Little bits of red burning coal would fly out of the locomotive and disappear. But soon after, he would feel dust settle on his arm as it rested on the window. He could see tiny bits of black charcoal on his arm and shirt.

Ravin could see many passengers sleeping at various angles when he glanced inside the carriage. Some were leaning forward and resting their heads on their knees. Many had their mouths open. Heads moved forward steadily little by little until a point was reached when the whole body was about to fall forward. Something would warn such forward swaying sleeping passengers, and they would recover and sit back, opening their eyes briefly, and the process would repeat itself.

Ravin could sense a slight drop in the speed as the train came within a few miles of Anaradhapura. The locomotive would also let off two or three hoots, as if to warn the stationmaster.

Little huts would begin to appear at long intervals, indicating that the train was approaching a township. Small signals and posts with numbers on them would begin to appear. A dog could be heard barking. Small railway bungalows would appear with lamps lit inside. Finally, three or four railway tracks with wagons and carriages parked on them would appear, and Ravin knew the train had arrived at Anuradhapura Station.

On arrival of the train, the activity on the platform would take on a familiar pattern. People would be getting on and off. Vendors would appear. Trolleys laden with cargo would move along the platform.

It would feel as if the train journey had been a long one but there were no signs of the morning appearing.

After Anuradapura, the train would speed on to Vavuniya. This station had a different feel to it. It was a smaller station, and the few vendors would be dressed differently. The vendors were Tamil people living in a rural Tamil area. Here, Ravin felt as if he had arrived in a different country. The faces looked a little different. The smells were different. The soil smelled damp, and the trees gave off a different smell. He would smell mango trees and gum trees. The men were dressed in vesties white cloths worn below the waist not in sarongs as in the South. Many people were bare bodied waist up with a cotton shawl thrown over their shoulders. The porters looked leaner. There were hardly any men in trousers. There were no women wearing cloth and jacket, which was only worn by certain types of Sinhalese women, housemaids and wives of farmers with little formal schooling.

The women in Vavuniya were dressed in saris of plain cotton. This meant that were all rural persons and wives of farmers.

In Vavuniya, vendors sold thosai – a sour pancake made with rice flour and ulundu, a type of lentils on a banana leaf. Tea and coffee was sold, but no bottled aerated water drinks, like cream soda or Lanka Lime, were sold.

Leaving Vavuniya, Ravin could see the popular Palmyrah tree appearing. This was exciting because, for Ravin, the Palmyrah tree made Jaffna different from Colombo. He felt he was now close to Jaffna.

Ravin could not see the sun yet. The lights from the train still formed a shadow that moved on a wall of shadows of trees and the brown earth. But some passengers had finished sleeping and were looking out with bright eyes as if the journey was coming to an end.

For Ravin, an interesting part of the journey was Elephant Pass, which was yet to come. The people who got on board at Vavuniya were now mostly standing in the corridors.

As the train moved on, some signs of dawn approaching would appear. The darkness would be a little less intense. The sky would appear at a distance as a pale blue patch, and Ravin would feel excited because Elephant Pass was not too far.

He had never seen an elephant pass. The days when elephants roamed that far north were over. What Ravin looked forward to was really the excitement of seeing the sea cutting into the land. Since they'd left Colombo, the train had kept inland. And now there would be even a bridge over which the train would cross the shallow sea. Kilinochi and Paranthan were the stations before Elephant Pass. Kilinochi was a small station. Very few people got on or off the train. The train did not stop at Paranthan. Only certain slow trains stopped there. The sand was white around the station, and the light was appearing clearly from the east.

As the train approached Elephant Pass, it slowed down and even stopped briefly, as if railway workers were checking the track before proceeding to the bridge. They were about to cross the Jaffna Lagoon. There were no trees, not even coconut trees. The sand was white as far as the eye could see. He could see coconut trees far away. The train crossed the bridge very slowly. He could see the water below the bridge. It was an interesting scene because there were no houses or vegetation of any sort. There were salt pans to be seen farther down. The sea was divided into plots, and each plot had water. The Salt Corporation collected the salt when the Sun dried the water.

But Ravin had never seen anyone working on a salt pan collecting salt.

After Elephant Pass, the vegetation returned. But the trees were different, and the Palmyrah trees were everywhere. It was open country. The train would stop at Pallai. The day had arrived, and the train was active with people getting on and off and conversation drifting around.

Ravin was looking forward to arriving in Jaffna, and it was now clear that they were close to Jaffna. Chavakacheri was a large station, and a large number of passengers got off the train. The name of the station was unusual. It meant Javanese quarters, the place where people from Java lived. But Ravin never saw Javanese. He could, however, see that many people in Jaffna had slightly raised cheek bones and round faces and were fair skinned.

The roads got busier as they got closer to Jaffna. Bullock carts of different shapes from those in Colombo, cars, horse carts, lorries, and a lot of bicycles were all stopped at the railway crossing waiting for the train to pass.

The sight of horse carts with shining brass fittings and horses with bushy tails excited Ravin. His sisters and mother would be up, and they would all strain to take a look at the horse carts. Ravin would request a horse cart ride from the station to the house in Vannarponnai. But he knew that a lot depended on Father rushing out early and securing a horse cart quickly. The carts were first come, first served, and the carter had preferences about the road and direction he would be taking.

There were porters, but just when you needed them they were busy carrying other people's luggage out.

If Ravin's family was lucky, they would be seated on a horse cart, straining to look at the horse as it waved its tail and trotted, clippety clop, almost putting Ravin to sleep with its rhythm.

The road was tarred. The colour of the sand on the road edges was whitish, for Jaffna was a limestone peninsula. The smells were different fresh and with a salty tang, for the sea surrounded the peninsula.

The people looked different. Hardly anyone wore trousers. There were no ladies in skirts going to work like in Colombo. There were no tall office buildings. Boys going to school wore short trousers and shirts. Girls wore skirts and blouses.

The houses were set back from the roads with Palmyrah or coconut palm leaf fences shutting off the houses from the roads. Some houses had walls. Ravin always noticed that the walls in Jaffna were whitewashed, unlike in Colombo, where the walls were always creamy or yellowish. There were grills in the wall sometimes. These houses were owned by better-off people like lawyers and doctors.

The shops looked different too. They were smaller and not many people were to be seen in the shops. They passed an in-ground water tank, the size of a small swimming pool, and temples, schools, and a small eating establishment.

When the horse cart turned into Navalar Road, some houses were recognisable. They had no Palmyrah or coconut palm fences. The cart passed the Navalar Press and then the small bookshop and stopped at Navalar House. Both buildings abutted the road with the walls rising two storeys, unusual for Jaffna.

To Ravin, arriving in Jaffna with its smell of the sea and unusual fragrances was not complete until he entered Navalar House and met Ravin's grandparents and aunties and then quietly walked into the back garden. To Ravin, this was a big garden with its fence of palm leaves at the bottom of the land. It also had two wells, one near the kitchen and one farther down for bathing and washing clothes. He looked forward to looking into the wells because each well had resident tortoises, and the large size of the well always fascinated Ravin.

Ravin's family was greeted warmly by the aunties and grandmother. His grandmother's smile was something he looked forward to. She always smothered him with kisses and hugs. Aunty Laxmi, married to Uncle Siva, would come down from upstairs.

Grandfather would come a little later, from the bookshop. A little back door opened from the bookshop into the house. He walked with one hand on his shoulder. He had an old stab wound scar on his shoulder going back to the days he was a custom and excise officer in Malaysia.

He had been stabbed during a raid on an illicit liquor distillery in Kuala Kangsar. A nerve had been disturbed on the shoulder and was causing pain in his old age. He had a leaf on his shoulder with oil on it prescribed by a native physician. His white long moustache would extend wide as he smiled. Ravin could feel the moustache tickling him when his grandfather kissed him.

Ravin's father's two sisters would come from a room on the side of the house. It was the prayer room, but it had carpets and served as a study room as well.

On entering the house from the road, one stepped into a long enclosed veranda with two large windows on either side and many chairs. On the right of the veranda was a room with a large table full of files. The right-hand side room was an office for Uncle Siva, who was a solicitor. The left-hand side room was a visitors' room with cane table and chair, a bed, and a cupboard called an almirah. Lots of photographs were hung on the walls of the veranda. There were pictures of Laxmi, the Hindu goddess of wealth, and Saraswathie, the Hindu goddess of knowledge. Laxmi was dressed in red, and the goddess of knowledge wore a white sari and held a lotus in her hand.

As one stepped further into the house, past the veranda, one came into a sitting room with a tall ceiling. This room had a cushioned settee and chairs. Photographs of Ravin's third aunty and her husband hung on the wall. He was a surveyor, and the couple lived in a small town called Yatiyantota, closer to Colombo. Photographs of other aunties and uncles, family group photos with grandmother and grandfather hung on the walls.

The walls were very thick, and cupboards were very deep and built into the wall. A glass cupboard displayed interesting dolls and miniature houses, a collection of items of interest.

A tall stool stood in one corner with a large square glass bottle, a crystal glass perfume bottle on display. Ravin liked to stand below the bottle and see the light through the bottle. It was the largest bottle he had ever seen.

A sheet of glass on the roof allowed the sunlight to fall into this room, which was really a vestibule plus sitting room, opening into the central living area. A staircase led from the vestibule to the rooms upstairs. The upstairs rooms were occupied by Ravin's solicitor uncle and his wife.

Stepping forward from the vestibule and sitting room, one came to the spacious area that was like an inner veranda with a large rectangular area open in the middle. There was no roof over the rectangular area in the middle of the house, and the sun lit up the second half of the house. Rain fell into the rectangular area. Ravin always looked forward to playing in the area open to the sun because it was below the level of the house, about two feet below with gutters draining in from the roof and water going out through drains. A wire mesh prevented crows from flying inside the house.

Built around this open rectangle in the middle, the downstairs had two bedrooms, a prayer room, a dining area, and a kitchen. If one walked into this area, there were only one or two chairs, but people sat on the floor on mats and cotton carpets. On the left were the doors leading to a bedroom and the bookshop. On the right were the prayer room and another bedroom. On the other side of the open area were the dining area and the kitchen.

"It must be holidays for you now," was one of the conversation openers. This was followed by, "Which grade are you in now?"

The tea or coffee would be served as refreshment. This was something Ravin was interested in because of the taste of the water. Tea, coffee, or water never tasted the same as it did in Colombo. Ravin's family never liked the taste of the water but got used to it within a few days.

Ravin's aunty, Padma, who was still doing studies at a higher level, would engage Ravin in conversation about what subjects he was doing. His other aunty, Rani, would stay closer to Ravin's grandmother, as they engaged Ravin's mother and sisters in conversation about news from Colombo.

The male cook took the family's suitcases and bags upstairs. Ravin's father would stay closer to his grandfather, and their conversation would be about books currently being typeset or printed and the books waiting to be published. Schoolbooks would be printed towards the end of the year. Some were written by Ravin's father and others by various known persons, the most well known of whom was Ravin's father's grand-uncle. Many of his books were prescribed as textbooks, and reprints were done every year. Sometimes Ravin's father and grandfather would disappear into the bookshop or the press next door.

After the conversation and the refreshments, Ravin's family would be asked whether they would like a bath. This offer would be quickly accepted, and Ravin's mother, sisters, and Ravin would take their clothes and go to the well. On the way to the large bathing well, they would linger at the kitchen well looking at the tortoises. The kitchen well was close to the kitchen exit door, and they could smell the breakfast being prepared. Lentils and rice flour pancakes with vegetable (sambar) soup with coconut sambal could be the menu. The cook would prepare the coconut sambal in a mortar and pestle.

Ravin and his mother and sisters would look for charcoal toothpowder made from rice chafe, the brown outer covering of the rice kernel. The chafe would be burned to turn it into a powder. They would find a little box with the black charcoal-like powder near the well. They would take a little bit of the rice charcoal powder in their palms, dip their index fingertips in the black powder, and polish their teeth with their index fingers.

Ravin's mother and sisters would wear long skirts. Ravin's mother's skirt would be pulled up to her chest to cover her breasts. Ravin's mother would send the bucket into the well and pull the heavy bucket of water out. The bucket was at the end of a rig. The pole would be balanced on little walls and have a stone tied at the other end, as a counterweight, so that it could swing up and down with a little manual assistance. Ravin and his sisters would line up and have the water poured on them. And while the children went to the side and soaped themselves, his mother would pour a couple of bucket of water on herself. The water was hard, and no bubbles came up when they soaped themselves.

The tortoises in the large well hid in the bottom when the bucket came down.

After the soaping and more buckets of water, they would use their towels and change to fresh clothes using the towels to cover themselves, like at the beach.

After the bath, the family would go upstairs to the room assigned to them. The room was large enough for the five of us. But we usually slept in the open living area downstairs on mats because it was cooler and the family conversations, with everyone seated on mats, continued into the night.

On hearing of the family's arrival in Jaffna, relatives came to meet them. Some would decide to spend the night.

Accommodation was not a problem since the open living area could sleep dozens of people on mats and carpets.

In the upstairs sitting room, Ravin liked to look at the various things collected there, especially the dolls from India kept in a glass cupboard. Sometimes Aunty Danalaxmi would open the cupboard and let him look at the dolls and curios inside it.

Of the three windows in the sitting room upstairs, the middle window always fascinated Ravin. It was really a tall door with bits of curved areas, and it went up to the ceiling. It must have been designed to open and allow furniture to be moved upstairs. The door was always locked.

The bedroom on the right had three windows. One opened out to the road. The second opened to the side where the press was. From here, Ravin would see the large gate and the drive between the house and the press. The press had thick walls and arched windows through which he could see the machinery moving and the printers working. The third window fascinated Ravin because it opened into the bedroom downstairs. The room downstairs had a tall ceiling since there was no upstairs room built over it. Looking down, Ravin could see the bed and almirahs in which grandmother and grandfather kept their things. Looking beyond the downstairs bedroom, through the bedroom doorway, he could sometimes see people walking in the open living area, passing the bedroom. He did not know that later, as a much bigger boy, he was to come and use this room to study, away from the distraction of Colombo. By then, Uncle Siva and Aunty Danalaxmi would have built their own house close by and moved out.

The second bedroom, normally assigned to Ravin's family, also had three windows and a bed. One window opened to the road, and the second window to the next-door house. One could see the roofs of all the houses on Navalar Road, up to the point where it met and crossed Kankesanthurai Road and even far beyond, where Navalar Road continued along its way. The third window opened into the downstairs prayer room.

Very large pictures framed in thick carved wood hung in the prayer room. They were pictures of Lord Krishna, Lord Siva, Lord Vishnu, Goddess Laxmi, Goddess Saraswathi. Incense and joss sticks burned slowly. Carpets and mats covered the floor. This was Ravin's youngest aunty's favourite room.

Having applied talcum powder on their faces, neck, and sometimes even hands and having combed their hair, they would go downstairs. The breakfast would be ready. Lentil soup and other vegetables dishes, like aubergines, potatoes, and tomatoes, and onion sambal would be served with pancakes or string hoppers or puttu, a crumble made of rice flour and coconut and steamed in a bamboo stick or steamer.

Ravin looked forward to string hoppers and puttu in Jaffna because they were dark brown, made from brown rice ground into flour. The taste was unusual and made a change from the white wheat flour preparation in Colombo. Brown rice, referred to as country rice, rarely made its way into Colombo.

The vegetables tasted different, and the spices tasted fresh. The cooking was a different style. The tea and coffee was made less strong and had a different taste due to the well water.

After breakfast, Ravin's mother and aunties and other ladies would sit around his grandmother. She would sit on a cane-woven chair, and the ladies would sit around her on mats or on the smooth cemented floor. It was a gathering of the clan on a small scale a time for quiet enjoyment for all ages.

Ravin enjoyed exploring the attic floor above the bookstore. He would look through the heaps of books that were no longer in demand and various bric-a-brac, such as an old gramophone with a dog painted on the voice producer shaped like a trombone. The words "His Master's Voice" were printed on it. Bits of old typewriters and other office machines were stored in the attic.

Parts of an old car were lying in the backyard. Ravin liked to sit on the mudguard and imagine how it looked when it was still working.

Many relatives lived close by. They dropped in to visit the new arrivals.

Ravin's Uncle Anandan asked him one day whether he had seen the Dutch fort in the town of Jaffna. Ravin said he knew about it but had not visited it. They went to the Jaffna Fort the next day.

It was an impressive building. The tall walls were built of blocks of granite. Some buildings were located within the fort; the ceilings in the church and offices were very high.

"This is the oldest colonial building in Jaffna," said Uncle Anandan.

"It is built with granite blocks, like the temples," noted Ravin, touching the wall of the Dutch fort.

Uncle Anandan pointed to the smooth granite wall and said:

"Local builders knew how to cut and assemble stone blocks. So they must have used the local experts."

They walked inside the old fort and saw the old church.

"The church inside the fort has nice woodwork," Ravin commented.

Uncle Anandan pointed to the roof and said:

"That is typical of the style used by the Dutch in their colonies. The Portuguese were here before, and we have some words like almirah, which we use even today in Jaffna. "

"Do we have a Portuguese Fort?" asked Ravin as they walked along the sandy yard of the fort.

"No," Uncle Anandan answered, explaining, "The area used by the Portuguese was taken over by the Dutch. Before the Portuguese came, the king of Jaffna had built a palace, which was torn down by the Portuguese."

"Do we have anything left of the old palace?" asked Ravin.

"No. The Portuguese were very violent. They were not like the Dutch. The Dutch were only interested in trading with the local people. The Portuguese were converting the locals to Christianity and wanted to teach the Portuguese language. That was why they took away the king of Jaffna and made him a prisoner. Sankili, the king, was killed by the Portuguese because he refused to cooperate with them. He made the mistake of punishing and even putting to death converts to Catholicism," replied Uncle Anandan.

"What happened to the Sinhalese king?" asked Ravin

"There were two other kings in the island," Uncle Anandan told him. "Both were Sinhalese kings the king of Kotte in the south near Colombo and the king of Kandy in the hill country. The Portuguese and even the Dutch and English after them, could not find their way into the hill country to imprison the king of Kandy, but they made the king of Kotte cooperate with them. The king of Kotte cooperated by ordering his followers to do what the Portuguese wanted done. He himself became a Catholic and changed his name to a Portuguese one to avoid the fate of the king of Jaffna."

"If the Dutch were more interested in trading, did Dutch ships come here to Jaffna?" asked Ravin

"Yes they did," his uncle replied. "Point Pedro was called Parithi Thurai before the Portuguese came. The Tamil meaning is 'cotton port'. So there was trading in commodities when the Portuguese came. The Dutch took over the trading activities. After all, it's only a short journey to Kanya Kumari in South India. Even small boats can make it. Jaffnapatnam was a centre of Dutch activities, and a thriving Dutch community lived there. Before the Portuguese, ships owned by the Jaffna kings sailed around."

"Did they trade with the Sinhalese?" asked Ravin.

"There must have been some trading. The cotton trade was a necessity in south and north Lanka because the cotton industry in Sri Lanka was not well established. Cotton spinning and cloth making was a big industry in South India, as it is even today. Traders and merchants must have travelled regularly taking local produce to South India and bringing back cotton materials."

"Was there any trading between the kingdom of Jaffna and the kingdom of Kotte?" Ravin wanted to know.

Uncle Anandan replied, "I am sure there was a lot of trading going on especially when the harvest was good and there was excess food or spices. Also brassware was popular in both areas, as were farming implements and farm animals. At one time, the king of Jaffna extended his territory far down south because there was no suitable king found in the south or some disagreement came up. King Ellalan, a Tamil king, ruled a vast area until the Sinhalese prince, Gemunu (also known as Dutugemunu) defeated him. Both fought on elephants, and when Ellalan died, Prince Gemunu built a tomb for him. All persons travelling past the tomb had to dismount and pay respect to King Ellalan (also known as Elara)."

"Dutugemunu is an unusual name," noted Ravin. "Gemunu or Gamini are usual names in the south."

His uncle explained, "The word dutu refers to a bad man. Dutugemunu meant 'the bad prince Gemunu'. Because he killed Ellalan, he was referred to as the bad prince. Ellalan was a popular king among both Sinhalese and Tamils. Ellalan was an elderly man. But he agreed to a man-to-man battle to save the lives of hundreds of soldiers on both sides. The young prince showed his appreciation and good manners by making people respect the dead king. This is why Gemunu ordered that everyone must dismount and pay their respects to Ellalan."

"So there must have been regular visitors between the north and south," Ravin noted.

"Yes. Not much was written about the trading though. Bullock carts were used then. But boats were much safer because of the thick jungle between the north and the south."

"Our train came through jungle for a long time," said Ravin.

"Yes. More than half the country remains uncultivated, especially in the north," said Uncle Anandan. "The north is where the Tamils are. But there are signs that the Sinhalese are planning to get these lands for their people. The law is very one-sided. The British laws made northern lands into crown land."

"Are you saying that Tamils do not own the lands?" asked Ravin.

"The Tamils lost out under the British. During Portuguese and Dutch rule, the Tamils had a separate administration. The Dutch did not impose their laws in the north. We had our separate administration. But the British unified the administration of the north and south. That's why we are having this problem now. This also meant that all the land in the northern Tamil areas became crown land," explained Uncle Anandan.

"Are you afraid that the Tamil areas will be taken over by the Sinhalese?" asked Ravin.

"No doubt about it," Uncle Anandan replied gravely. "We can see it happening already. The Mahaweli Development Scheme is already bringing Sinhalese rural people into the north and east. Take Amparai it was a Tamil area, but only a few Tamil people lived there. But it's now a Sinhalese area under the government's resettlement scheme."

"Do you think that this a deliberate plan? Or is it that there is much vacant land in the north?" Ravin wondered.

"I think it's a plan the old man, the first prime minister, devised. You can't blame him. The British handed over the powers to the Sinhala majority race. It's also true that there is much land in the north that could be used for cultivation. The young boys in the north fear that more and more land will be taken over. That's one of the reasons they are rebelling," said Uncle Anandan.

They returned home. Ravin wanted to go the Dutch Fort again when they came back next holidays.

***

After about a week of staying with their father's family in the Jaffna suburb of Vannarponnai (which meant the place where the washer women and men used to stay) Ravin's mother would say that they needed to go to Uduvil to visit her father. This was an exciting prospect because they could visit many village houses and meet many smiling relatives, visit the farms with their wells, visit Maruthadi market, go to the Green Memorial Hospital in Inuvil, visit Kankesanthurai with its lighthouse and the crowning glory, and bathe and swim in the warm spring pool in Keerimalai.

The trip to Uduvil was usually by horse cart. Sometimes Ravin's father would borrow a bicycle and follow them. Uduvil was about seven kilometres away from Vannarponnai. If they went by hire car, father would return to Vannarponnai in the same car after staying for a short time. He had some of his work in the printing press all the time.

The various landmarks, such as the Marunarmadam Santhai (santhai meant "market") were pointed out as we travelled along the road, which was a tarred road. The gravel on the side of the road was always white because the Jaffna Peninsula was mostly limestone. As they got close to Uduvil and passed the Green Memorial Hospital (where the American missionary, Dr Green produced his first batch of medical graduates in 1838), names would be mentioned:

"This is where you turn off to go to Aunty Selvam's house," Ravin's mother would say.

"This is where my aunty, Dr Ponnamma, worked," Mother would say.

On arrival in their portion of land in Uduvil, they were greeted at the gate by Raman, the young lad adopted by Ravin's grandmother and grandfather. He was from the tea estates in the hills. He would be delighted to see Ravin. When Ravin was a small boy, he would immediately carry Ravin on his shoulders and do a celebratory jig. Our grandfather hurried out of the house. It was about fifty metres away from the gate. There was a stone house, which had begun but had not been completed, between the gate and the house Ravin's grandfather lived in.

Ravin and his family loved the open veranda of the house their grandfather lived in. It stretched the full length of the house. Three rooms were set in a row and two had beds. The veranda ran along the bedrooms and stretched beyond them, and the thatched roof was held up by seven or eight wooden posts at the front and a brick wall at the back of the house. Between the posts at the front of the house was a low parapet about two feet high. The chairs in the veranda were set in a row, as if in a little resort hotel. Some could sit on the low veranda wall and others on the chairs. Male visitors and children tended to sit on the veranda wall, but visiting ladies came in and sat on the chairs.

The house had no well for water. Water came from their grandfather's brother's house, situated opposite on the other side of the road. A tortoise lived in the well at their granduncle's house. They always looked forward to seeing it when they went to the well in the morning and then in the evening for their baths. After their baths, they walked over to the house our granduncle lived in. It looked quite different from grandfather's house. Goats were tied to trees, and Ravin and family could pet them and rub their backs and feed them leaves. Ravin and his sisters would request them to milk one of the female goats. The granduncle's children would show

53

Ravin and his sisters how it was done, and the milk squeezed out would be sent to grandfather's house. There were two bulls and a cow. The children could touch them and feed them with grass and hay.

The children enjoyed lifting the cover of the huge mound of tobacco, which was the size of a hut, and sniffing the tobacco smell. It was being cured and being made ready for the market.

When they have had breakfast, Ravin's favourite position was to sit in the veranda on the low wall and tie two ropes to two trees immediately outside the house and hold them as if he was the driver of a bullock or horse cart.

The food was always different in Uduvil. The rice was red rice, the unpolished variety. The vegetables were delicious, cooked with different ingredients. The water tasted different. The tea tasted different because of the water and the way the water was boiled. The wood fire and smoke from the firewood made a difference. The coconuts were plentiful, very cooling and always available. Nongu, the fruit of the Palmyrah tree, was also delicious. There were three sections in each Palmyrah fruit, each the size of three or four grapes. You ate the fruit by inserting your fingers in the pulp and digging the pulp out. The pulp looked like the pulp of a coconut when it was still soft the drinking coconut. But it tasted very different; the flavour was very distinctive. The family's favourite was pooran, the shoot of the fruit of the Palmyrah tree, when it was left to germinate in the ground. The Palmyrah was well suited to the dry climate. It was also popular for use in house construction, especially for use as rafters for the roof.

The mango trees were everywhere and provided low branches to sit on. The children would sit on low branches, and mother would sit on a mat below the tree. Ravin was not allowed to go to the top of the tree, although he did sometimes climb all the way. Some trees were easy to climb. He plucked a few mangos while up on the tree. Sometimes there were large red ants, and he was careful not to disturb them. When it was afternoon, the family took mats and slept under the tree.

One of their favourite relatives was Papper, their granduncle's son. Papper always smiled a shy open smile, and his teeth were a brilliant white. He used to take the goats to graze in the mornings. They would be tied to a new grazing area near their farm, about ten minutes' walk away from the house. Some of the goats were allowed to wander around the roads, eating leaves growing on trees lining the roads. The trees were part of the fence made of woven coconut or Palmyrah palm. The trees formed posts for the fencing. These wandering goats had a stick, about a meter long, hanging from their neck, parallel to the ground, and held by a rope around their necks. This stick was long enough to stop the goat from walking through open gates and entering other peoples' gardens.

One of the family's favourite morning outings was the visit to the fields. They had to leave early to the fields to make sure that they could see the watering of the fields in the morning. The well for the fields was large, and three men were getting the water out of the well. A large post was used as a lever to take the large bucket down into the well and bring the water out. It was always amazing to see a man walking up and down on the lever holding onto a rope. When he walked towards the bucket at the end of the lever, the lever dipped down into the well and filled the bucket with water. When he walked on the lever away from the well, the bucket came up from the well, and another man turned the bucket of water over into a water channel. The third man tended to the channel, diverting the water to various parts of the field. Men were out in the field weeding and making sure that all the plants got water. There were chillies, onions, aubergines, tobacco, tomatoes, and other vegetables growing. Sometimes, the bulls were in harness, ploughing parts of the fields. Ravin and his sisters enjoyed the smells of the red earth, with the water entering it and creating a different earthy smell.

In a compound close by lived Kannan, the toddy tapper. The compound was the property of an extended family of toddy tappers, considered to be of low status because of their occupation as toddy tappers. He was a fair-skinned man. He and his wife and children visited Ravin's family during their stay in the village in Jaffna. Kannan was bare bodied and wore his coconut and Palmyrah tree climbing clothes, the cloth wrapped around his loins like a heavy bandage, leaving his legs free of clothing and allowing him to climb trees to tap toddy. On his hips, he wore a belt with pouches for the knives, some curved, for use when cutting the Palmyrah or coconut palm fronds at the top of the tree, where the toddy collected in clay pots.

The manner in which the visitors spoke, the distance they kept, and the words they used conveyed a sense of respect for Ravin's family. After they had gone, Ravin's mother would explain that the visitors were of the Nalavar caste, considered to be of low social status in the community because of their work. Supplying toddy to the drinkers was not a noble trade, unlike being a farmer. Being a farmer was a noble pursuit. But most families had educated their children, and the educated ones were in Colombo and all over the country, working in offices, teaching in schools, and working in hospitals. Ravin's mother's father himself never tilled the soil, moving away and working in the tea estates and learning how to make tea and rising to being a tea estate superintendent in Kotmale when the British still ran the tea estates. But his two brothers stayed in Uduvil village, tilling the soil and growing tobacco and vegetables and looking after cows and goats.

It was the same with Ravin's grandfather. He never tilled the soil either. He had his education in Jaffna and went away to Malaysia and worked in the British government service as a customs and excise officer, earning enough money to return to Jaffna and set up a press and bookshop.

But being a farmer was the gold standard. Being a fisherman was a little bit better than being a toddy tapper or a dhobi (a working class person providing a clothes laundering service). Even being a metal-working class person (thaddan) was of low status. But being a jeweller, a skilled worker handling gold, was an exception, and the trade was well regarded.

The caste system showed up with the lavatory system in the town. The carriers of night soil (Pariah caste) were ubiquitous in their services in the town. After all, in the village there was no need for the services of this night soil working class. Pit toilets were quite satisfactory in the village. The town night soil service a bucket service was paid for by each householder.

Ravin's aunties, Rani and Padma, asked him about his studies and what he would do when he grew up. Ravin had no burning ambitions, and simply going to university was the name of the game. He had no ambitions to be a farmer. Indeed, looking around in Uduvil village, it was clear that only those young men who were poor at studies were the ones who were going to take over the family farm. The size of the farm hardly ensured sustenance for all the children. Some members of the family, those without much academic ability, married into families in the Vavuniya and Vanni areas. This ensured a larger farm and a better income.

Ravin's mother would be discussing and planning their favourite trip, the trip to Kankesanthurai and nearby Keerimalai, where spring water collected in a small swimming pool. Arrangements had to be made to get a buggy cart and the two bulls to pull the buggy cart. At a pinch, the two bulls owned by Ravin's granduncle could be roped in.Raman the family's household help, would try to get another bigger pair of bulls from one of the neighbours. These bulls were bigger and faster, and the family could spend more time paying calls on people and swimming and less time on the roads. Raman doubled as the carter for the trip.

Finally, the arrangements would be complete, and they would all be seated in the cart. It looked quite different from the bullock carts seen in Colombo. The roof of the cart jutted forward to allow the carter to sit at the front edge of the cart. Ravin would be allowed to sit by the side of Raman, like a co-pilot. Raman would have the whip and the ropes in his hands. When the road was clear, Ravin was allowed to hold the rope and prod the bull gently with his toes, like Raman did. Ravin would watch Raman get more speed out of the bulls by tapping their rear legs with his foot. The bulls would move faster for a while and then get back to a steady trot. Every now and then, Raman would touch the bulls' balls with his toes. This resulted in a very fast rush every time, almost an all-out dash. He reserved such spurts for the occasions when there was no other traffic. Cars were rarely seen. When seen, they were all either Austin Somersets or Morris Oxfords with an occasional Ford Anglia.

They passed Maruthadi market, the biggest market close to Uduvil. They sometimes stopped to buy vegetables, rice, bananas, betel nuts, betel nut leaves, and vegetables to cook in Keerimalai or take along as presents. On rare occasions, one could see fish, but meat was never seen in that market. Meat was rarely consumed in the peninsula. On festive occasions, family groups might jointly purchase a goat for slaughter and distribution.

Passing Green Memorial Hospital always made Mother talk about her relative who was the first woman to go and study overseas. She became a doctor in Edinburgh. Dr Green was an American she would say. He came as an American medical missionary and set up a medical college. He learned Tamil and translated medical books into Tamil in 1838. He taught medicine to several batches of Jaffna medical students who were awarded Boston degrees.

Sometimes they stopped over in Manipay to meet up with relatives of their father. This was a chance to rest the bulls and give them a feed and water. The hay for the bulls was carried under the cart in hessian bags. Manipay houses were in brick and had large gardens. The menfolk would be away at work. The aunties would be pleasantly surprised but would insist on making the family a snack and sharing cups of tea or coffee or aerated waters. The mangoes served were always the best in the island and grew well in the peninsula. A car would be parked sometimes, and Ravin would take the opportunity to note its details, like the shape of the lights, wheels, steering wheel, mudguards, and bumper bars.

Inside the house, were interesting collections of dolls, paintings, brass oil lamps, spittoons, and trays. Most interesting to Ravin were the pedal cars, which were no longer being driven, as the children were grown up. When he was young enough, he was allowed to ride them. When they left, there would be more mangoes, coconuts for drinking, and limes and vegetables in the bullock cart.

The road to Keerimalai was flat and straight. Palm trees lined both sides of the road. The palm trees had fruits. They were a type of date palm with smaller fruit. The travellers plucked some fruit and ate them as they moved along.

The sight of buildings and signs of activity would signal that Keerimalai was close. On arrival, they would first arrange lunch, for there were no eating places. One had to arrange for cooking of lunch with one of the houses. Travellers could overnight in these places for a modest fee.

Ravin and his family would be dropped off close to where the warm water springs were. Walls separated the women's section from the men's sections. When Ravin's father came along, he would make a float from two coconuts tied together, and they would swim in the men's section, with the floats supporting Ravin so he would stay afloat. Raman would join them after tying the bulls and leaving the animals in a shady area, munching their hay and resting. The water was blue like sea water, but it was warm, and one could see the water bubbling up in one corner of the small bathing pool. The sand at the bottom of the pool was pure white, contrasting with the blue water. When Ravin was young, he would go to the ladies pool as well and swim with his mother and sisters. The ladies wore sarongs tied above their breasts.

When they were tired and hungry, they would walk out and go to the place where lunch had been arranged. They might finish their vegetarian meal and fruits and lie down on the veranda or sit against the wall for a rest while the sun grew less hot. Raman would be in command as he had to time the trip. When he said he was ready to move, they would get into the cart and move away. The ride to Kankesanthurai was not too long. They would reach Ravin's uncle-in-law's house by midafternoon.

Ravin's uncle and his wife lived in the hill country. The relatives would be delighted to see them, as they rarely came to Colombo. A meal would be prepared quickly of fresh vegetables and lentils. Amazingly, even though they may have had three meals of the same vegetables during the day, each tasted different. The spices used and the method of cooking were different. At the end of the meal, betel nuts were chewed with betel nut pepper leaves and lime.

The highlight of the visit was a visit to the lighthouse at Kankesanthurai. Ravin's uncle's father-in-law was the lighthouse keeper, and they were lucky to be able to climb some way up the lighthouse and look around. They never got to the top.

They would leave in the late afternoon, and the bulls would be urged to dash frequently with prods to their legs. The bulls would raise their tails and move into a run. After a minute or two, the bulls would slow down to a clippety-clop. Occasionally, they would push out dung, and their tails would drop down and swish around.

When they got close to Uduvil, and they left the tarred roads and entered the lanes, darkness would fall, and a little lamp was lit on both sides of the cart to warn cyclists of the moving cart. They would ride through the last few lanes in darkness and arrive in Uduvil tired and ready to sleep.

Their holidays seemed to pass very quickly. When the time came to return to Colombo, the family was not looking forward to returning to their home.

Arriving in Colombo, they felt they were strangers, coming to a strange place. Everything was different in Colombo. The place smelled different, the people looked different, the streets looked different, and the climate felt different.

Seeing familiar places and things like new motor cars, women in attractive dresses, and men dressed in smart trousers and long-sleeved shirts gave Ravin a pleasant feeling. This feeling was also mixed with a sense of fear because of the thugs who seemed to rule the streets of some parts of Colombo. Many carried knives and walked in a menacing way, with their sarongs raised, defying the rules of decency and morality.

Chapter Three
The Hill Country

R avin's family visited their relatives in Nawalapitiya when
they did not go to Jaffna during school holidays. Ravin's
mother's elder brother lived in Nawalapitiya and worked in
the Urban Council. He had gotten married recently. Ravin
looked forward to going to the hill country because of the
cool climate, the hills and mountains, and the interesting train
journey.

Ravin's father never joined them on these holidays in the
hill country. Maybe it was because of the lack of space for
many people in the small house.

The train journey to Nawalapitiya was more exciting
than the journey to Jaffna in some ways. The train had first-,
second-, and third-class coaches. The coaches they sat in were
third-class coaches but were always in a better condition than
the coaches taking them to Jaffna. The passengers were also
quieter and less talkative. Some coaches had silver hand basins
for taking a wash. The toilets were clean and looked like they
were for second-class passengers. Ravin could not remember
seeing any first-class coaches.

The first part of the journey followed the familiar route
through Kelaniya, heading north from Colombo. After this,

the train took another route, and the stations were different and the smells and noises in the stations very different. The people dressed differently. They were all Sinhalese. Men wore coloured checked sarongs and shirts and wrapped their hair in coloured cloth. Most women wore coloured sarongs without checks and a short top that ended at the waist, leaving a small gap between the top and the sarong. Some women wore the sari but in a different way, with one end of the sari fanned out in front and the other thrown over the shoulder in the usual manner. The sari-clad women were from well-to-do families and travelled with children and servants. Men travelling with these ladies wore trousers and shirts.

Some people chewed betel nut during the journey. Occasionally, they had to get up and spit out through the window. The train would stop at stations every half an hour or so, and new passengers would board at each. Some would stand. The entrance to the carriage was open, but there were no seats at the entrance. Three or four passengers could enter through the entrance at the same time but had to move into the compartments where the seats were.

The train was very long, as some carriages were going to Kandy, where the train line ended. The others carriages were going to Gampola and then to Nawalapitiya and onwards to Nuwara Eliya and many other places.

Most stations had canteens. People got out and had tea or coffee and ate buns and snacks at the canteen. Passengers with families chose to sit in the carriage and buy tea, bananas, buns, and cakes from vendors, who carried these items in trays and walked alongside the trains. The tea and coffee was served in drinking glasses.

Ravin's mother rarely purchased tea or coffee. Sometimes, she purchased aerated soft drinks like Vimto, orange, lemonade, cream soda, or lime two bottles to be shared between the family. The bottles had to be returned to the vendor, who remembered to come back to collect them. Sometimes, he waited close by to collect the bottles before moving along the train. We spoke to the vendors in Sinhalese. Our accents were different from the accents of the Sinhalese. Having lived in Colombo all our lives, we spoke Sinhalese quite well. Some of our neighbours only spoke Sinhalese, and many of the shopkeepers and street vendors of fish and vegetables spoke only in Sinhalese.

At one of the stations, an additional steam engine joined the train. The train was now being pushed from behind and pulled from the front. It was exciting to see the two steam engines working, and Ravin and his sisters craned their necks to catch a glimpse of the two engines. Little bits of coal flew out of the engine and landed on their faces when they put their heads out to look at the engines. The smell of coal burning came along with specks of coal. Passengers hair smelled of coal even when they did not put their heads out. Everyone took turns sitting at the window. When Ravin's mother's turn came, Ravin's younger sister sat on her lap, getting her turn along with the mother. Sometimes, they managed to get two window seats opposite each other, and Ravin, being the eldest child in the family, would get a window seat.

The train had begun to climb, and the engines made a lot of noise, bellowing noisily as they moved slowly. Many men were now close to the big entrance, enjoying the views of the hillside down below the tracks as the train was now moving very slowly, almost at walking pace. The train moved close to the edge, about one yard separating the track from the slope of the hill.

Approaching Kadugannawa, the train moved at a snail's pace, the engines straining to move the coaches uphill. There was a corner around which the train inched along, and it was worrying. Some men got off the train at this point and walked faster than the train. Either they were going to the front of the train, or they decided it was easier to walk to their destinations. Maybe they had no tickets and did not want to stay on the train until it reached Kadugannawa Station.

When the train reached Kadugannawa Station, there was much activity, lots of passengers moving around, some taking a break from sitting in one place. The vendors were very busy, as there had been no refreshments for over an hour. The train had been on the move for about three hours, but it seemed a long time. Finally the train took off, and now the train moved much faster as the difficult climb was over.

On reaching Peradeniya, the train split, and the front coaches headed for Kandy with one of the engines, while the rear coaches went towards Gampola and all the other stations pulled by the second engine. There was a lot of shunting in Peradeniya to split the train into the two. The links connecting the coaches were disconnected, and the front coaches moved forward by the front engine to another track to allow the second engine to go forward and then reverse to get in front of the second set of coaches.

Seeing the engines move up and down and reverse making very unusual sounds, two or three bellows to move two or three yards, was exciting. When the engine connected with the stationary coaches, the coaches moved back a few feet, and a lot of noises came from the links and stoppers connecting the coaches.

The train moved along valleys and hillsides, and the cool breeze made everyone feel cold. Ravin's mother covered her hands in her sari. It was almost too cold to put one's head out and look at the scenery. When the train went around a bend, one could see the scene in front of the engine, and Ravin enjoyed looking at the scene before the engine. The views were better when they were closer to the engine. After the train split up at Peradeniya, their carriage was now closer to the engine, but there were more bits of coal landing on their faces. Bits of coal landed well inside the carriages. White clothes showed the bits of coal on the clothing. Some got inside the eye and had to be removed. Ravin's mother fashioned a wick out of the corner of her sari to remove any coal bits out of the corner of the eye. Ravin could do it too by using the corner of a handkerchief. The trick was to move the bit of coal to the corner of the eye near the nose with the corner of the handkerchief and then move it out.

As the train moved towards Nawalapitiya, there were more up-country Indian passengers on the train. These passengers were easy to identify by the way they dressed and the quiet way they moved. The ladies wore their sarees in a different way. The saree did not fully cover their shoulders. And the cloth was of a cheaper quality and colours of the saris were different. The men covered their heads with woolly caps and wore cardigans. Covering the head was useful in the colder hill country. They never spoke on the train and were very restrained in their movements.

"These tea estate people are very quiet people," said Ravin to his mother.

"Yes. That's how they are brought up," said his mother. "Very humble people. Also don't forget, they are living in a foreign country, among people who could chase them out."

"But they have been living here for over a hundred years," said Ravin.

"Yes. But they know their place in society," his mother explained. "They are tea estate workers. They are called coolies, which is the lowest status in the country people who only do tea plucking and lowly jobs."

"That's why they seem to be so quiet. They don't want to be noticed," concluded Ravin.

Our mother sometimes spoke to the ladies if they sat next to her or opposite her, especially if they were Indian Tamils. "Where are you from?" she would ask.

If the town or tea estate mentioned was known to her, she would mention the names of some persons she knew who came from that town or area.

If they both knew the person mentioned, it would signal the beginning of a new friendship or connection between the two of them.

Many times you heard, "I met so-and-so, and we attended so-and-so's wedding," or words to that effect.

This would mean that Mother and the woman had mutual friends but were only meeting for the first time. If the conversation continued, the children would engage themselves in watching the passing scenery.

Names of other persons would be mentioned, and it would at least be acknowledged that either Mother or her new friend had heard of such a person but had never met him or her.

"It's good that we met on the train today. If I come to your town, I will drop in to see you," they would say to each other.

The train's arrival in Nawalapitiya signalled the need to bring down suitcases, which were placed on the rack above the passengers. If there were young men in the carriage, our mother would say, in Sinhalese, Tamil, or English, depending on how the person looked, "Could you kindly help us to get the suitcases down?"

If anyone was getting his suitcase down, the opportunity was taken to request that the person get our suitcases down as well. Often, they stood on the passengers' wooden bench seat to move the suitcases out and make it easy to pull the suitcase down. Sometimes the suitcases were made of metal. This would mean that one had to be very careful, and people sitting below would be asked to move out of the way to enable the suitcase to come down.

There were porters available to help with carrying the bags and suitcases. They would come onto the carriage to get the baggage down and take it outside. They had trolleys and could push them outside to where the carriers and cars were. Compared to Colombo Nawalapitiya had hardly any cars.

Ravin's uncle would be at the station. Everyone smiled. Mother had sent a telegram from the Kotahena Post Office, near St. Lucia's Church, informing her brother of our arrival the next day. Very few people could afford telephones. Uncle had come with a man to carry the big bag. While Ravin and his mother and sisters carried the smaller items, the carrier placed the big suitcase on his shoulder and made the short walk along with the family to the house.

Aunty, who would have prepared refreshments, would be waiting for us to arrive. She always cooked a delicious meal with fresh vegetables and brown rice. The family all agreed that her style of cooking was excellent and different from all the others. Her sothy, a sauce made with coconut milk, onions, chillies, and spices was a speciality from Kankesanthurai, her home town in the north. When Ravin and his family visited Kankesanthurai, their aunty's father prepared the same sauce.

It was afternoon. A bed was prepared for the family to have a nap. Mother went for a nap, but the children were more interested in looking at the scene from the front of the house. The kitchen was at the back of the house, separated from the house. Two or three metres of open space separated the kitchen from the house, and a drain ran along the edge. Water was stored in a drum in the open space for bathing. A drain took the water away. Water ran along the drain and went outside the house. The toilet was separated from the house, beyond the kitchen. To go to the toilet, one had to open a small gate and walk outside. It was a bucket kept by the Urban Council and paid for by the occupant of the house. Small children were allowed to sit on a potty in the open space where the water pipe and water drum were kept.

Uncle often spoke about the Urban Council, where he worked. He would talk about the member of Parliament for Nawalapitiya, Mr Jayatilleke. The parliamentarian would come to the offices and discuss matters he was interested in. He would ask about the road works and council construction work.

Uncle also spoke about the chairman of the Urban Council, Mr Ratwatte. Mr Ratwatte would also be interested in the progress of the contracts, and Uncle would talk to him. Uncle always talked about the various visitors to the offices he worked in. Most were well-known persons and businessmen in Nawalapitiya.

Ravin, being the eldest child and a boy, was allowed to walk outside the house and along the road towards the main road. Within fifty feet from the house, he could see the train tracks down below. It was a drop of about thirty or forty feet. People walked down to the train tracks and along the track towards the villages between Gampola and Nawalapitiya. Ravin was not allowed to walk too far towards the villages.

The girl who lived with them and did a lot of household chores came from one such village. She was adopted by Ravin's grandmother as her parents wanted her to be taken to live with Ravin's grandmother in Colombo. Her parents had many children, and it was the practice that some children went to live with better-off persons trusted by the parents. The children were treated as part of the adopting family, going out with family on visits and to the cinema. The girl's older sister had also been given to Ravin's grandparents to be brought up. She was a nanny to Ravin, carrying Ravin and looking after him when his mother was away at school teaching. The two girl's brother had also been sent to Colombo to be brought up in Colombo. The boy attended school for a year or two and then dropped out. He stayed at home, and his main chore was to go shopping for food items at the market and the shops. Later, when he had grown up, he was found a job at the small soap-making factory. He learned to make washing soap and pack the soap bars into boxes. He went back to Nawalapitiya when he was in his twenties.

Ravin took walks along the road to the town area. Coming out of the street, he would pass the tea cider factory, which could be seen from to the house, and come to the railway crossing. If the gates were closed, he would wait with the others, even though some men would creep under the gates and walk across the track to get to the other side. The train would come very slowly because the railway station was very close. It was always thrilling when the steam engine came past, with smoke billowing up and steam coming from pistons near the track. It was a big black steam engine, with engine drivers covered in coal, the guard standing and looking through his special glass panes from the last carriage carrying the cargo. This view of the steam engine and carriages was much better than looking at them at the station.

Once the train had passed, the lorries and cars started moving again. Ravin walked along the road and passed all the shops. Sometimes he walked past all the shops and came to open fields where rice was growing in small plots.

People in Nawalapitiya looked different. It seemed like it anyway. They were village people. Even the shopkeepers looked different, like village people. They dressed different it seemed. Many had woollen head covers, especially the Sinhalese villagers. They wore vests, and their shirts were buttoned up. In Colombo, the people who wore sarongs left many shirt buttons open at the top, and many tied their sarongs once around their waist and once again folded their sarongs from the bottom and tied it around their legs, showing their legs and knees. It was meant to allow the legs to keep cooler and also to help with walking faster. People who wore sarongs or vesties and ladies wearing saris and cloth faced the problem of having to lift their garment slightly with one hand when wanting to move fast, like rushing to catch a bus.

Ravin's family looked forward to their evening walks. When their uncle came from work, he would have a cup of tea, and they would all start an evening walk after locking the house up. They avoided the town centre and walked along the other roads and went up steps cut on the hillsides leading to houses on the hillsides. Some of the roads were not sealed. They were wide enough for cars and trucks. One of the roads led to a riverside and a house close to the river. They stopped by to visit the family living in that house. The family were of Indian descent and spoke in Tamil. The accent was different, and Ravin's mother would adopt the accent. The accent and the words were familiar to Ravin. The family were delighted to see the visitors, and they smiled profusely and laughed loudly, expressing a sense of great happiness in seeing the visitors. They served biscuits, Indian snacks made from lentil flour and tea. Ravin slipped out after having his tea and inspected the garden and surroundings. Sometimes, there was a dog to be petted. The children played with the dog. The really friendly dogs walked up to all the visitors to be patted on the head.

If Ravin stepped out into the garden, his mother told him not to go too far. Ravin walked along the gardens, as the flowers in Nawalapitiya were different and looked very fresh because of the cool climate.

One of Ravin's mother's favourite friends was a family that lived on a hillside overlooking the railway station.

A highlight of the stay in Nawalapitiya was the visit to the cinema. One road led to a slight hill where the cinema stood. Excitement filled the air as the children were allowed to walk up to the balcony and sit and watch the Tamil movie until the visit was at an end. The balcony seats were very expensive, and Ravin's family had been in the balcony on very rare occasions. They usually sat downstairs in the middle of the cinema. The cheapest seats were in the front and called the gallery. These were for manual workers on low wages. Right at the back of the cinema, below the balcony, were the most expensive seats except for the balcony seats.

They walked every evening when uncle came after work. Their walks were in different directions on each occasion.

71

Often, they stopped at a friends house for a chat. Ravin understood that, even though his uncle took regular walks, he rarely visited friends. When Ravin's family were there, his uncle would make it a point to stop over at a house so that Ravin's mother could catch up with friends.

During one of his morning walks, Ravin discovered a chekku mill. Here, the millers made oil by pressing sesame seeds in a stone mill drawn by two bulls. The bulls went round and round, with the pole resting on their necks. At the other end of the pole was the stone mill, a circular stone about a yard in width, resting on another circular stone, which was stationary. The sesame seeds were poured through a hole at the top of the stone, and the oil oozed out into a large bucket from a hole in the circular stone below. Ravin felt sorry for the bulls, which had no choice but to keep moving round and round. He had seen mills in Colombo, run by electricity. Huge belts connected the electric motor to the mill. The men poured dried chillies, dried turmeric, cumin, and other condiments into the tray at the top of the mill, and the powdered condiments came out at the bottom into buckets and trays. He had never gone into the copra mills in Colombo, near Kotaboam Street on Grandpass Road. As a child, he had seen the steam-driven trucks with smoke coming out from the funnel carrying copra in bags made from coconut rope. These steam trucks brought copra to Colombo and parked outside the mills waiting to be unloaded.

Another highlight of his visit was a visit to one of the Tamil families from Jaffna. They had a daughter who was extremely pretty, rosy cheeked, and fair skinned. She was about ten, close to Ravin's age. Ravin loved to look at her face, especially her eyes, which were clear, and lips, which were pink, almost red. During his walks, Ravin often walked past this house, hoping to see her standing at the door. But he never did.

As the holidays came to a close, there was some talk of getting tea from one of the tea estates. Certain types of tea from tea estates were regarded highly. People working in high positions in the estates were able to get this type of tea without labels and wrapped in tin foil at a nominal price.

There was coffee too. It was a finely ground coffee, brownish in colour with a strong aroma. The coffee bought in Nawalapitiya tasted different. It was purchased and packed ready for the return to Colombo. Now, Ravin and his sisters were thinking of the return journey.

Local vegetables and plants were packed in cardboard boxes for the return journey. Ravin's mother had asked her friends for flowering plants that were rarely seen in Colombo.

A feeling of sadness would come to Ravin as the train left the station bound for Colombo. He also felt a little excited to think that he would be meeting up with his friends and playing cricket and football, walking along, and spotting their favourite girls.

CHAPTER FOUR
THE PEACEFUL PROTEST

The government of Solomon West Ridgeway Diaz Bandaranayake had announced that it would be passing an act that would make Sinhalese the only official language in Ceylon. The Tamil-speaking population had protested, and the Tamil members of parliament had announced a silent protest, in the way Mahatma Gandhi did. The silent protest was going to happen in front of the Parliament, on Galle Face Green. This news made Ravin worry because Colombo had a lot of thugs. Ravin later found out that the protest had been stopped using thuggery. He gathered information about how the day had proceeded.

The Galle Face green was free of strollers, for it was six o'clock in the morning. The sea was calm and its colour a blend of blue-green and grey. At the southern end of the green were two cars parked, close to the Galle Face Hotel.

About an hour later, six cars arrived within a few minutes of each other and parked on the northern end, near the Parliament. Several men emerged from the cars. They were all dressed in white long-sleeved cotton shirts without collars. Their bodies from the waist to the toes were covered by a long white cotton cloth, something like a sarong, tied tightly at the waist and hanging loosely at the feet.

They were talking excitedly, standing on the edge of the Galle Face Green. The Galle Road was only a few yards away from where they stood. Galle Road separated the Galle Face Green from the low walls on the grounds of the Parliament building.

Some of the men from the group began to sit on the Galle Face Green, looking towards the Parliament. Some mats made from the leaf of the palm tree were taken out of the cars and spread on the green. The men arranged themselves in two rows, and they faced the Parliament.

About an hour later, a crowd had assembled to look at the men seated on the mats, dressed in the long white cotton loose clothing. More men in long loose cotton clothes arrived and joined the others on the mats.

The sun had risen and rays of sunlight shone on the men seated on the mats. Some of them were sweating. One man, bald and round, seemed to be sweating profusely. He was a member of Parliament. Another member, the lean frail grey-haired man seated next to him, seemed to be more comfortable.

The two cars parked at the southern end of the Galle Face Green, near the Galle Face Hotel, started up and drove along Galle Road. They slowed down as they neared the Parliament and came to a stop on the roadside. Four men came out of the second car and walked towards the group seated on the mats. Two of the four wore dark sunglasses and cotton hats. One was tall and well built with handsome features. The second man in dark glasses was short. His face looked long, and he had a receding chin. The four of them came closer to the assembled onlookers.

After watching the group on the mats for a few minutes, the four men walked back to their car. When they reached their car, three men from the other car came out to meet them, and they spoke for a few minutes. The three men got into their car and drove away. The two men in dark glasses got into their car. The other two stood outside, leaning on the car.

A police vehicle arrived and parked a little farther away from the group seated on the mat. An inspector with a peak cap and two policemen walked towards the group on the mat.

"Good morning," said the inspector.

"Good morning," replied the bald fat man.

"Are you going to stay here much longer?" asked the inspector.

"Yes. We will be here for many days," replied the bald man, "as long as we need to."

"I cannot permit this," said the police inspector. "We will have to take you to the police station."

"But we have given notice of this assembly as required under the Public Assembly Act," answered the frail grey-haired man.

"I am not aware of it. But you can see that there is a crowd gathering here," said the inspector.

"Let the crowd gather. We want people to know about our protest," replied the bald fat man.

"I know you are staging a protest against the Official Language Act. But I cannot do much if there is a problem here. We might not be able to offer you any protection," said the inspector.

"You are by law required to protect lawful acts of protest. That is basic part of a democracy," said the frail grey-haired man.

"I am going to report the matter," replied the inspector. Turning to the policemen, the inspector said, "Go to the car and radio the superintendent."

The policemen walked towards the police car.

The crowd around the group seated on the mats seemed to be expecting some outcome from the police. The policemen came back and told the inspector that the superintendent wanted him to come to the station.

The inspector turned and walked away towards the police car. Three more policemen got out of the car, and the inspector drove away. The four policemen stayed away from the crowd surrounding the protestors.

It was past ten o'clock, and cars were arriving at the Parliament building. A small group of members of Parliament were looking towards Galle Face Green from between the pillars of Parliament.

A few minutes later, a lorry pulled up near the car that was parked early in the morning near the Galle Face Hotel at the southern end of the Galle Face Green. This was one of the two cars that had moved closer to the group seated on mats, facing Parliament.

Two by two, men got off the lorry. They were dressed in sarongs and shirts, and many had handkerchiefs tied around their necks.

About twenty-five men were now standing near the lorry looking towards the group seated on mats. The second car, which had gone away, returned and parked close to the lorry. The two men in dark glasses and hats got off the car, and the group of men who had arrived by lorry turned to face the two men in dark glasses.

The tall fair-skinned man spoke in Sinhalese. The group from the lorry immediately walked away down the green towards the crowd and the group seated on mats. The men in glasses stayed back.

The crowd shifted about and made room for the men who came in the lorry. Some people moved away and left the scene. The group from the lorry moved closer to the group seated on the mat. One man with a scar on his face seemed to be saying things and was leading the group from the lorry.

The four policemen walked closer to the crowd, noticing that a large group was coming out of the lorry and moving towards the crowd.

The man with a scar on his face stood in front of the group seated on the mats. The four men from the lorry stood around him. "Your people must go from here," he said in Sinhalese.

The fat bald man seated on the mat replied. "We are not making trouble here. We are seated here silently." He answered in Sinhalese.

"We want you to go now. If not, we will chase you from here," said the man with the scar on his face.

"We will not go from here," said the frail man haltingly. "We are seated in front of the Parliament. Our country is a democracy, and Parliament protects peaceful protestors."

Suddenly the man with the scar on his face lunged forward and pushed the grey-haired man over and started kicking him. The entire group from the lorry rushed towards the seated men and started kicking them. The fat bald man tried to fight off his assailant, but three or four men surrounded him, and blows fell on the man's face and blood spewed out from his nose and lips.

"We are going to murder you now. Bring the knives from the lorry," shouted the man with the scar on his face.

At this point, the people seated on the mats were talking to each other. Two were helping the grey-haired man walk towards the cars parked on the edge of the green. All of them gathered their mats and followed. Some had bloodstains on their white clothes. They walked past the policemen, who stood silently.

The group from the lorry were shouting obscene words and making rude signs with their fingers towards the group walking away.

Ravin read about all these happenings, and visitors to Ravin's house gave more details.

Chapter Five
Sundays

It was a clear Sunday morning, and Ravin wanted to go for an early swim. He changed into his shorts and shirt and wore his swimming trunks. He folded a towel into two and rolled it to make it easy to carry in his hand. He walked over to Tony Ahmadeen's. Tony's sister came out and asked him to sit while she called out for Tony. Tony came out a few minutes later, with towel rolled and ready to go. The boys walked down towards the Foreshore Police Station and waited for the bus. The bus came along, and they sat down. The ticket collector came to collect fares, and each paid his ten-cent fare to De La Salle School. The bus passed along the harbour, turned left, drove along the shops, and turned right and climbed up the hill. The bus stopped just after passing the top of the hill. This was the closest bus stop to De La Salle School in Mutwal.

They walked downhill towards the beach. De La Salle School was on a hill, one of the few hills in Colombo. Mutwal had all the hills in Colombo, but the other hills were far from the sea. De La Salle Hill was the only hill close to the sea.

The Fishtails Club was built below De La Salle, on the slope of the hill sloping into the water. The clubhouse was open. Lokka, the caretaker, was away. Ravin and Tony changed in the changing room and came out and jumped in the water. The water was cool but not cold. They swam along the beach about a hundred yards away from the beach. The water was calm, and they kept a good pace. They swam up towards the fisheries harbour, which was marked by a series of large rocks going out to sea. When they reached the rocks, they turned back towards the club. The distance was about a quarter mile. They swam up and down eight times, and it took about an hour and a half. When they came out of the water, they were tired. They showered and sat on the chairs.

It was still too early for the Sunday swimmers to arrive. They pooled their money and paid for a bottle of Lanka Lime aerated water and shared it between them. They talked about the coming two-mile swim in Mt Lavinia. They were training for it. The hot favourites to win were training in Mt Lavinia, but the bus fares to go to Mt Lavinia were too much. The journey to Mt Lavinia took about an hour each way, and without being members, going and changing in the Mt Lavinia Club was a hassle. But leaving clothes and money on the beach while out swimming was a problem.

Sometimes, senior members of Fishtails came to the club to have a few drinks and chat. Unlike the well-known clubs, Fishtails was a refreshing change, with its simple bar, simple food, and simple people. When the famous two mile swim or the surf carnival were coming up, some Fishtail members would offer to take the swimmers out to Mt. Lavinia so they could get used to swimming in the strong surf. This was such a Sunday.

Ananda, who owned a well-known family tea business and lived in Cinnamon Gardens, had come all the way and was ready to take the boys to Mt Lavinia for a training swim. Two other members with cars were ready to provide transport as well. The three cars drove out of the club and headed for Mt Lavinia. The boys did a good days training in the strong surf of Mt. Lavinia.

Ravin's studies went on as usual. The weekend arrived. Saturday was Ivor's day for roaming around, and he had cycled to Kotahena from Wellawatte. When he arrived in Ravin's house, Ivor was sweating profusely and asked for a glass of water. Ravin and Ivor sat in the sitting room on the wooden chairs with woven cane on the bottoms and backs of the chairs.

Ravin's mother walked in and talked with Ivor. "Did you cycle all the way?" she asked.

"Yes. I came through Galle Face and Fort," said Ivor.

"It must have been tiring. How's your sister? It's been a long time since I've seen her."

"She's fine," replied Ivor.

"I'll get you something to drink," she said, getting up.

As usual, tea was served.

"Let's cycle around a bit," said Ivor.

"All right. Let me get ready," said Ravin, getting up and going into the room. Some of his clothes were hung up in the almirah cupboard. He got into his clothes, and the boys cycled out of the compound.

"Who is that girl?" asked Ivor, seeing a fair-skinned girl walk along the road.

"She is one of the Arnolda girls," said Ravin. The Arnolda family lived on Pickerings Road and owned two garages; one was next door to Ravin's house.

"Very nice. Has she got a boyfriend?" asked Ivor.

"Don't know. Lots of boys visit the family," said Ravin.

They cycled along towards the harbour and joined Kotaboam Street before turning right towards Mutwal. They passed the tobacco company, and soon after, the Protestant church came into sight. It was nice to turn into the church and sit on the steps, looking into the harbour, for awhile.

"I always enjoy this view, Ravin," said Ivor.

"I agree. It's very peaceful, and nobody disturbs you," said Ravin.

"Who lives in the houses?" asked Ivor, looking at the well-designed and well-kept houses behind the church.

"People working for the Port Commission," said Ravin.

"Now that the Sinhala Only Act has been passed, I'm not sure I want to look for a job in this country," said Ivor.

"What are you going to do? Go to England?" asked Ravin.

"Yes. I am working out how to do this. Being a Catholic and a Tamil is a double burden now. My brother says that, already, the promotions are restricted to Sinhala Buddhists. The Chief Archaeologist, who was an Englishman, left the country, but the man who should have succeeded was sidelined because he was a Burgher Christian," said Ivor.

"Some Tamils are now taking on Sinhalese names because they feel safer that way," noted Ravin. "The doctor in Colombo is a Tamil in fact, the certificate hanging on the wall gives his name correctly but he has changed his name to sound like a Sinhalese name."

After resting for a few minutes, the boys headed back towards Kotahena and St Anthony's Church. Passing the church, they took the road alongside the harbour, the road made of blocks of stones. The bicycles bounced on the blocks. A lorry came along, and Ivor hung onto it and moved along without peddling. He let go of the lorry after about a mile, close to Khan Clock Tower and waited for Ravin. Ravin did not get a lorry to hang onto, and it was too risky for two people to hang onto one lorry on such a narrow road.

They rode past the clock tower and headed towards Lake House and then went past the Houses of Parliament and headed towards Galle Face Green.

Passing the Galle Face, they stopped near the church.

"Let's stop at Alerics," said Ivor.

"But I only have two rupees," said Ravin. Two rupees was good enough to eat two vadas and two dosai and drink tea and still have one rupee left. But ice cream at Alerics could cost more than one rupee.

"That's okay. I have money. But we won't buy knickerbocker glories, only ice cream," said Ivor.

They parked their bicycles and sat down at a table near the road. It was nice to lick your ice cream and look at the passing scene. They watched motorcycles like Gilera and Moto Guzzi, Triumphs and BSAs and girls dressed in skirts that had buckrams holding them up like floating skirts. The Galle Road was where you could see the latest styles in clothes, hairstyles, push cycles, motorcycles, and cars. Occasionally, a bullock cart passed along loaded with coconuts, lending a piece of rural reality to the city scene.

Ravin and Ivor got back on their bicycles and rode towards Bambalapitiya. Reaching Buller's Road at Bambalapitiya Junction, they passed the Majestic Theatre, a cinema. It was showing South Pacific, a Hollywood musical.

"This is a good film, Ravin. We must go and see this next week," said Ivor. "Let's stop at my brother's house," he added. "And then let's get Nada and go for dosai at the Saras," said Ivor.

They pulled up at Duplication Road and went into Ivor's brother's house. Ivor's brother was there, and the brothers fell into a conversation while Ravin walked through the garden, which was full of lovely flowering plants and was tended nicely. Ivor came out and called Ravin.

"Let's go now and meet Nada. I hope Vasanthi comes out," said Ivor. Nada's sister, Vasanthi, was a firm favourite of Ivor.

It was almost midday when they rode into Dickman's Road and stood at Nada's gate. Vasanthi came out to the veranda, went in, and sent the household help to come and open the gate. They wheeled the bicycles into the driveway and parked them along the wall. The Peugeot 404 was parked in the garage. That meant Nada's father was in. They sat in the veranda, and Vasanthi came out and spoke to Ivor, much to his delight. She always teased him about which girls he was interested in.

When Nada came out, he was wearing his sarong and vest. Vasanthi said goodbye and went inside, much to Ivor's chagrin.

"Where have you guys been?" asked Nada.

"I went to Ravin's house in the morning. We went up to the church and then came through Galle Face, stopping at Alerics," Ivor told him.

"Sounds like a good round. Are you guys going swimming?" asked Nada.

"No. Maybe it might have been a good idea. Next time we should bring our swimming trunks. We could go to Kinross for a swim," said Ivor.

"I like a good swim at around this time," said Nada.

"Let's go for a dosai feed," suggested Ravin.

Three bicycles took off, and the boys went to Galle Road through Dickman's Lane. They rode up to Saraswathie Lodge Hotel, which was a South Indian vegetarian eating place.

The dosai feed was up to usual standards. The dosai (lentil and rice flour pancakes) were fresh, and the sambar (lentil sauce with vegetables) was good. The sambal (coconut, onion, lime, and chilli) was up to standard. The vadai (lentil doughnut with chilli and onions) was hot and tasted delicious. The tea was served in stainless steel cups and saucers. The bills were left on the table by the waiters.

After paying their bills, the trio got on their bicycles and crossed the road to the other side of Galle Road and slowly rode up to the beach, passing Greenland's Hotel. The bicycles had to be left lying on the sand as the lamp posts and walls were too far for propping up against them. Leaving bicycles far away was too risky, even with the band-shaped lock clicked on. The side stands of the cycles sank into the sand, and they fell over after awhile.

"What's news of Siri?" asked Nada.

"The family went to the home town, Matara," said Ivor.

"Godfrey is getting ready to go to England," said Ravin.

"Lucky fellow. What's he going to do?" asked Nada.

"He is going to do A Levels and go to university," said Ravin.

"He's all right for money. His parents are going to pay for his trip," said Ivor.

"I guess if we do A Levels here, there is no guarantee we can get a place at university," said Nada.

"The chances of a university place are ten to one," Ivor pointed out.

"Best to find a good job," said Nada.

"That's almost impossible," said Ravin.

"Unless you have a well-connected relative who can arrange it. It's who you know that matters. Some guys are all right if they have businesses to work in, like Rex. His family has their store in Pettah, and he doesn't have to worry about finding a job" said Ivor.

"I guess a lot of the boys can find jobs since they come from well-to-do families. But we are going to have to do well in the examinations and get good results," said Nada.

"You can get jobs with GCE Ordinary Levels. Some guys like Manuel are working already," said Ivor.

"You're talking about jobs as clerks and such like. Our parents are expecting us to go to university and get better jobs," said Nada.

"I guess our parents are pointing to doctors and engineers and lawyers and saying those are jobs we should be aiming for," said Ravin.

"That's right. Nowadays, the opportunities are good for accountants. I met a person who came back from England recently. He qualified as an accountant in the UK. He is already holding a top job at Browns," said Nada. "He's a single man and lots of marriage proposals are being made," he added.

"I don't think I want to get into a proposed marriage," said Ravin.

"Depends on the girl being proposed," said Nada.

"I don't think we need to argue on this. None of us, including Siri, are in a job. We are not even qualified for a job," said Ravin.

"We are not even at university, and we are struggling to get notes to study for University Entrance. Chances of our getting into university are ten to one. As for me, I want to get to England first," said Ivor.

"Even that involves studying and passing exams. Nobody in my family has the money to send me to England," said Ravin.

They could see Siri riding towards them on a bicycle. "Hi, guys," he called as he came to a stop. "We came back today from Matara. I went to check in on Ravin. He wasn't there, and I went to Nada's. When Nada's family said you guys went out together, I dropped in at Saraswathy Lodge, and then I knew you guys would be here."

"How was your trip?" asked Ivor.

"Good. Met some friendly girls from the village," said Siri.

"Lucky guy. Look at us, just sitting and talking. Get anywhere with the girls?" asked Ivor.

"Village girls are very friendly. You get a chance to squeeze their boobs, and then they run away. If you stay for awhile, it's all right. You get a chance to do the real thing. Next time, I will go during college holidays," said Siri.

"Take us with you," said Ivor, and they laughed. Taking Tamil boys to a Sinhalese village would raise eyebrows. It could be done if the occasion was a wedding or a ceremonial occasion, like a school opening or hospital ward being extended.

It was getting towards evening, and some people were taking a walk along the beach and the beachside road. Families were walking along, going on visits and strolling, and enjoying the cool of the evening.

"Let's have some tea," said Siri, and they adjourned to Greenlands Hotel.

Once seated at the table, they could see the doughnut-shaped vadas and other lentil-based snacks being served, and they decided to order them along with the tea. Families came to Greenlands so they could eat out. Upstairs rooms, where the tables were more attractive, were available for groups. Vegetarian meals with rice as the base were served here along with the snacks. The meals were cheap and suited everyone's purse.

"There is a rumour that some politicians are going to use thugs to make trouble for Tamils in Colombo," said Ivor.

"Is this about what happened in Parliament?" asked Siri.

"Well they had a meeting in Jaffna and decided to perform satyagraha like Mahatma Gandhi. This was to ask for a federal constitution," said Nada.

"I guess Bandaranayake government is ready to pass the legislation. It's the opposition that's stopping it," said Ravin.

"The Buddhist priests and influential people in the villages are against the federal idea," said Siri. Being a Sinhalese person, he knew more about what was happening in the villages.

"The opposition is taking the opportunity to become popular and topple the government," said Nada.

"Well, Bandaranayake took the opportunity to make Sinhala the only official language and topple the United National Party (UNP) government. So now it's now the UNP's turn to topple Sri Lanka Freedom Party(SLFP) government using the same tactics" said Ivor.

"Anything can happen. Buddhist priests are powerful in the villages. Everybody listens to them, except maybe some educated people of standing like doctors, teachers, and well-to-do people with their private income from plantations and shareholdings," said Siri.

"Well-to-do people who owned their houses and had private income would vote UNP anyway," said Nada.

They finished their meal, picked up their tabs, and paid at the counter.

"I guess it's time for me to go. It'll be dark by the time I get home," said Ravin, getting on his bike.

By the time he reached Kotahena, the sun had set, and he had a wash and got ready for the night.

Ravin's mother was at the table correcting some examination papers. She taught various subjects, like geography, history, and Tamil at the Good Shepherd Convent.

Ravin stood by her side looking at the pile of answer papers.

"Can you arrange them according to the marks they got, with the highest marks at the top?" she said.

This enabled her to check her marking and see whether all got fair marks. Ravin arranged the marked papers, placing the highest on top. Some of the girls' names were familiar to him. Their surnames were the same as some of his friends at school.

He remarked, "Winifred must be a relation of George Wanniappa, who is in my class."

"She is his cousin," his mother said.

"How do you know this?" asked Ravin.

"She told me that her cousin, George, is in the same class as you at St Joseph's," said his mother.

"Maybe George told her that I sit next to him in class," said Ravin.

"Maybe. Some girls know about you. They talk all the time. I scold them and tell them to stop chatting and read their books," said his mother.

Ravin arranged the papers and noted the names as he filed them. He knew quite a few of them from their names, although he'd never met any of them. Some lived in Kotahena, and he had seen them. Only one was to his liking, a Gujarati girl who sometimes visited their house to see his sister, but he was too shy to speak to her.

Ravin's father arrived soon after. He often came late after giving private tuition and then visiting people. He was dressed in the normal way white shirt and white drill trousers. Most teachers came to school in white. Some wore a white drill coat as well. Ravin's father sometimes wore his white drill coat, especially if there was going to be a school assembly.

Ravin's father changed and went to the dining room. He sat down and served himself from the dishes covered and left on the table. Sometimes, he would ask for porial – fried potatoes and onions – and the girl would work fast and get it on the table very quickly. He was a vegetarian and non-vegetarian food was only cooked for Ravin's grandmother. She would only eat with fried fish or curried prawns. Dried fish and dried prawns were kept in the bottles as a fallback in case the fish sellers did not come to the house due to shortage of fish at market. The family, including Ravin's grandfather, was vegetarian.

Ravin's grandmother was a Christian, a Methodist. She always took Ravin to church in Jampettah Street. It was a Dutch built church, but the service was in Tamil. Ravin's grandfather was proposed to his grandmother as a suitable match even though he was a Hindu because he had held a good position in the upcountry tea estate. He had worked his way from tea maker to superintendent and was regarded as a tough disciplinarian. Grandfather Sinniah was a staunch Hindu and refused to convert to Christianity to get married to Grandmother. But his family persuaded him because it was going to be an "exchange" marriage; he was going to get married to my grandmother and his sister, Sellam, was going to get married to my grandmother's brother, an apothecary. An apothecary was regarded as a medical doctor in the village of Uduvil and all other villages. Doctors were very few, even though Dr Green, an American medical missionary, had set up a medical school in Inuvil (close to Uduvil) and graduated a few dozen doctors in the 1840s.

In the end, grandfather was baptized and took the name Samuel Sinniah. The wedding was held in the church, as was insisted on by Ravin's grandmother. But having complied with the demands, Ravin's grandfather never went to church again. The two children from the marriage, Ravin's uncle Rasiah and Ravin's mother were not baptized. When Ravin's grandmother argued with Ravin's father, she ended up calling him a heathen and the whole family a bunch of heathens. The arguments were usually about money.

Grandmother used to lend money to Ravin's father and mother and expected it to be returned with interest. She was good to Ravin. She would give him money and not expect it back. When he went out on his bike, he would ask for ten rupees from his mother or his grandmother. His grandmother gave him money to buy tyres and tubes and batteries for the bicycle lamp when his mother had run out of money. He rarely returned the money.

When the end of the month came, Ravin's grandmother expected all her loans to be returned. When Ravin's father didn't return the money he'd borrowed by the end of the month, grandmother called him a pariah, at the end of the argument. In turn, he called her a money lender.

Ravin's father sat in the sitting room reading newspapers until it was time to sleep. Sometimes he got up early or in the middle of the night and started writing. His favourite topic was the history of North Ceylon. He wrote short books on the history of Ceylon, which were published as readers for children in the lower school. It was about the ancient Sinhalese kings and the tanks, palaces, and dagobas they built. The battle between the Tamil king Ellalan (Elara) and the Sinhalese Prince Dutugemunu featured in them. He researched records kept in the museum and the archives and wrote about the lifestyles in Sri Lanka during colonial times. The life of Navalar, who rebelled against the colonial system, was one of his favourite topics. Navalar went to a Christian school and translated the

Bible into Tamil but later rebelled against the colonial ways and became a Hindu educationalist.

Ravin's mother said that Ravin's father's writings were a waste of time because most of the writings could not be published. Ravin's father did not have the money to have them printed. Ravin's grandfather could print them without charging, but money for the paper was hard to find. Occasionally, when a book was recommended by the education department as classroom textbook, there was a demand for it and there was no problem printing and stocking the book in bookstores. Ravin's grandfather had a bookstore between the press and the house. But Ravin's father travelled to Kandy, Nawalapitiya, and farther afield to deliver books for sale.

On Saturdays and Sundays, many visitors called in. Ravin's parents were raising funds to renovate a school run by Hindus at the waters meet in Mutwal. At the school, lessons were given and religious songs taught at weekends. Ravin was excused as he was studying for examinations. His friends were also studying for examinations.

Ravin wanted to go to a library to study for the examinations. The closest one was the public library near the town hall, but the British Council had a very nice library in Fort in the centre of the town area. He ended up at the British library, reading his notes and looking at some books. One of his subjects was Ceylon history, and any book on the subject seemed all right to read. He read a book by Father S. G. Perera on the history of Ceylon at the time of the arrival of the Portuguese. The book was easy to read and confirmed what his uncle had said. The king of Kotte heard of the Portuguese putting the king of Jaffna to the sword and wasted no time in converting to Christianity and taking a Portuguese name. Many of his courtiers converted as well and took Portuguese names like Perera, Diaz, Bastians, Fonseca, Fernando, and Almeida. The names have persisted, although many prominent people changed their names to

Sinhala names when the tide turned and Britain, the colonial power, granted independence to Ceylon.

Ravin's musings went back in history. Prior to the arrival of the Portugese with their guns, Ceylon's history seemed to consist of powerful families gathering armies and fighting over who should be king and who had access to the trading vessels and the traders who came from India and the Middle East. From India, reaching Ceylon was a simple one-day sailing trip to Mannar. From the Middle Eastern ports, reaching Ceylon required many days of sailing. The Muslim traders could not have brought silk and spices because these were available in India, much closer to Ceylon. Rather, the Arab traders wanted silks from India and spices from Sri Lanka so they could take these goods to the Middle East and then to Europe. Spices drove the Portuguese to come to India and Sri Lanka. The Muslim traders must have brought brass lamps, Middle Eastern jewellery, European furniture, and similar items to exchange for what was available in Ceylon, possibly gems. Muslims conversions happened along the coastal areas. There was little about what incentives were offered to convert to Islam jewellery perhaps or building good houses. Poor folk would have been tempted to become rich folk with houses and jewellery. Hambantota, the town in the south of Ceylon, means the place where the hambayas lived. Hambaya was the Sinhalese word for a Muslim. This town must have consisted of Muslim converts converted from poverty and Buddhism to Islam and prosperity.

Ravin's thoughts strayed while his mother continued correcting the answer papers. It appeared that, the people of South Ceylon tolerated the conversions from Buddhism to Islam and Christianity, while those in the north maintained opposition to these conversions. It was King Sankili's punishment of his subjects who converted to Christianity that led to his demise at the hands of the Portuguese. The swords of the king of Jaffna were no match against the guns of the Portuguese. Perhaps the king of Kotte, who lived near Colombo, was too far away to take any action against the conversions that were taking place in the deep south.

When she finished correcting her school papers, Ravin's mother asked him where he had been. He said he was at Bambalapitiya Beach with Ivor, Nada, and Siri.

"You have to study hard," she told him. "Your friends have no problems. It' will be easy for them to get jobs. And they have properties. But we have to study hard and find jobs. Take our landlord, Gomez. People like Gomez and Bandaranayke come from big families with plenty of money and lands. They are all right. You must know that we are struggling to make ends meet. As Tamils from Jaffna, we have little pieces of land and hardly any water. You have seen how our relatives in Uduvil village live a frugal life. Their only hope is to study hard and find a good job."

"You are always criticizing the Burghers too," said Ravin, "and the Muslims."

"Burghers drink too much," his mother answered. "Look at our neighbours. They are not even Burghers. Just because they are Christians, they are free to drink liquor every day."

"But they are just ordinary people," Ravin said. "They like a glass of toddy to feel better."

"Look at Mahatma Gandhi, Jawaharlal Nehru, Radhakrishnan, and Sarojini Devi. Or look at Bertrand Russell. These are great people, and we must try to be like these great people, not like these cheap people drinking smelly toddy and playing cards all day. What kind of life are they leading? Disgraceful. I don't want you to be like these drunkards."

Ravin had no ready answer, but it niggled him that she was winning the argument. After all, Mahatma Gandhi used to look for poor people's huts to sleep in when he travelled in the country. He wanted to show solidarity with these common people. And great men advised people to treat everyone as equals, as brothers and sisters. Also all races were the same in the eyes of God. At that time, Ravin did not know that the Koran laid down a different rule, that all non-Muslims were infidels and should be eliminated.

"But look at all these sarong johnnies on the roads," said Ravin. "They are working as labourers and getting little money. Their children can't get any education. They are lucky to get some food."

"These are men who never went to school, coming into Colombo and trying to get work. When they get their pay, they spend it all on drinking and smoking. Do any Tamils do this? Even a Tamil coolie will save and send his child to school," his mother retorted. "Tamils will eat rice and vegetables and save the money for education. Tamils are God-fearing. Sinhalese Buddhists don't believe in God. Lord Buddha only told them to meditate. Do any of these rascals meditate? That is why these fellows are thugs. They will rape and kill without hesitation. They do not have a conscience."

Ravin could not rebut what she said. There was a ring of truth to her words. "Buddhist priests are there to guide these uneducated Sinhalese," he said. "They go to the temple and pray."

"Lots of Buddhist priests I know are corrupt," she replied. "Many have women and pretend to be good men. They get money from donations, and nobody knows what happens to the money. They conduct prayer meetings, but people bring food and donate again. I don't trust them. I guess becoming a Buddhist priest is one way of progressing in life. You can't blame them."

"Some are good priests. After all, you were treated by a Buddhist priest," said Ravin.

"That's true. There are some who are real Buddhists. They meditate and lead a good life. But many see this as a profession one way of getting on in life and getting rich and powerful. All the politicians kowtow to the priests. Priests should not be involved in politics. Soon they will even contest elections and enter Parliament," said Ravin's mother.

"If you feel like this, why are we all living in Colombo? Why don't we go back to Jaffna?" asked Ravin.

"We should all go back to Jaffna, but what would we do? We need jobs. We can't all make a living on a small piece of land. A lot of Tamils like us, who don't know how to farm the land anyway, are living in Colombo. We are now part of this city," she replied.

"We have the Federal Party wanting a federal constitution. People leading the Federal Party want to live in Colombo but still want to have a part of Ceylon designated for Tamils," said Ravin.

"What's wrong with that?" she asked. "After all, they passed the Sinhala Only Act, which said that Sinhalese will be the only language used by the government."

"Well this is not going to happen. The courts have declared that the act was unconstitutional," he replied. "But I agree that the Constitution could be amended to allow Sinhala Only. The minority rights clause could be removed. So the situation for Tamils is going to be very difficult."

"I agree, but we must try," she said.

She placed all her papers in her file, and the file went into her bag. It was time to go to sleep.

***

Ravin cycled to college and parked his bike at the bicycle parking place, a long shed with a metal fabrication underneath where the front wheel of the bicycle slotted in and the bicycle stood up and you locked it.

At the Upper Six Arts, which had an uninterrupted view of the Beira Lake with its Kottam trees and chicken wire fence in places, it was business as usual. Mr. Kuruvilla had a morning class, and the class was considering the merits of the writings of D. H. Lawrence. This was the most exciting class for Ravin because here was a chance to read at least bits of the world's most infamous book, banned in every country. The class was only getting the expurgated version of Lady Chatterley's Lover, but it was still exciting. The four-letter words were all removed, and it would be many years before Ravin came face-to-face with the real thing, four-letter words and all. As a mature man, he was not at all excited by reading the four-letter word describing the sexual organ of a woman. The use of this word seemed perfectly normal in the context of the writing. In fact, it seemed the only word that would fit the occasion. But as a young lad, trying to spot where the omitted words might be while reading the book was a fruitless task.

Ravin listened to Kuru reading Lawrence's words out loud. Most of the students were attentive to Kuru's reading , but some sounds of whispering could be heard, and Kuru looked up from the book. The room went quiet again. Ravin remembered how Kuru used to call up boys who were talking and twist their ears. This disciplinary method was very effective and never led to any canings.

Ravin had felt the sting of Father Noel's cane for arriving late. He had even felt Father Marjez's less stinging cane. Father Marjez did not even bother to remove his Jaffna cigar from his mouth. He carried out his duties even though this part of his duties as deputy principal was not to his liking.

It was Father Marjez who gave Ravin a book from the shelf in his office called On Going to University by Sir Ivor Jennings. Reading the book, Ravin came across the expression, Corpore sanum, incorpore sanum. It meant "healthy body, healthy mind." Ravin was already doing a lot of swimming, and it seemed like he had already taken the advice offered.

Father Timothy was always fair; he always said, "Hold out your hand," and the sting did not seem to last as long as the one that was felt on the leg. But Ravin and his friends were seniors now and beyond the cane. Verbal stings were more common now. Even Kuru's ear twisting was rare at this stage of school life.

Father Peter Pillai did come into class during his rounds along the corridors. He was looking for unattended classes and mischief at the back of the class and along the corridors. Boys left out to kneel while the rest of the class made its way through the lesson were questioned by the rector and sometimes taken to the rector's office and given a strong dose of good advice and even a dose of the cane. If the teacher was late, Father Peter might come in and sit on the teacher's chair and test the student's knowledge while everyone waited for the teacher to arrive.

Whenever he asked a question and the student answered, "I have no idea, Father," he would say, "Don't say you have no idea. I'm sure you do. Just say that you don't know." Ravin knew that Father Peter had two doctorates, but he did not know what subjects the father had studied. Rumour had it that the father held one degree in science and the other in theology.

In later life, Ravin would remember Father Peter Pillai every time he came across carpentry tools like a wood saw. It was Father Peter Pillai who'd made sure everyone got a little carpentry and metalworking experience while still at school. The twinkle in Father Peter's eyes and his boyish smile contrasted with his girth and the robe he wore.

The history teacher, Mr. Rajapakse never failed to have notes to dictate to the students. None of the books seemed to contain the material he gave. He must have been drawing from what he'd learned during his University days. History of England by Trevelyan was such an entertaining textbook that Ravin had no difficulty with English history. But the book said little about the intermittent wars with Scotland. Maybe they were not wars but just raids by the English to take borderlands and push the Scots further into the north of the island.

Ravin's thoughts went to the conversations with Ivor and some of the others at St Joseph's. Ravin mentioned to Ivor the rather poor account of the Scots and the Irish given in Trevelyan.

"They were conquered races, with no colónies," said Ivor.

"I suppose it's a bit like Ceylon history," said Ravin. "Nothing's said about the Scotsmen of Sri Lanka, the Tamils. Ancient history also ignores Veddahs the true owners of the lands."

"It also seems that the Tamils did not undertake the building of tanks and temples like the Sinhalese," said Ivor.

"There are no rivers in the north to build water tanks. But certainly there were plenty of Hindu temples. I guess the population was too small to need big waterworks. The dry, almost barren limestone that is the Jaffna peninsula does not produce enough wealth to be spent on grand buildings, except temples" said Ravin.

"I guess this is a bit of a mystery," Ivor said. "Don't forget that Sinhalese kings had Rajakarya all the citizens had to devote a portion of their time each year to building public works. This meant that free labour was available to the Sinhalese kings. In Europe, this would be serfdom, and serfs had to give free labour to their masters."

"There must have been some pretty good buildings in the north," Ravin said, "at least a palace for the king of Jaffna. But the Portuguese took a strong dislike to the king of Jaffna because he beheaded converts to Christianity. They certainly took Sankili out. Nowadays these happenings are called something else foreign policy and is done by the US and Britain. And the Portugese must have taken any trace of his existence out by flattening the palace."

Chandran and Harry joined Ravin and Ivor.

"Did you know that somebody put sand in Ratnam's car?" asked Harry.

"Who did that?" asked Ivor.

"Nobody knows," said Harry.

"What are you guys talking about?" asked Chandran.

"We were talking about Ceylon history why there are no palaces in the north," said Ivor.

"But there are no palaces in the south either," replied Chandran. "I've never heard of one. Never heard of one in Kandy either."

"Maybe the Portuguese or the British demolished them," said Harry.

"Come to think of it, only North India has palaces, with each area being ruled by a raja. The people of North India cooperated with the European powers. Only a few tried to fight against the Europeans, but they had no answer to the European guns," said Ravin

"The Portuguese came with guns, and there was no arguing with them," agreed Harry. "Everybody shut up and did as they were told. In the south, in Kotte, very few were shot."

"It was the same in India. The guns kept everybody quiet. All the rajas cooperated. I guess by the time they could get guns smuggled along the silk route, the scene had changed. Trade had become the main thing. But the British Raj employed its army and navy to police the colonies," said Ivor.

"The colonial system took raw materials out of colonies like India and manufactured goods in factories. We are reading about it right now," said Ravin.

"The colonies supplied cotton and wool for clothing manufacturing," added Ivor. "They grew tea, coffee, and cocoa and sent the goods to Europe. The raw materials came back in nice packets, like Lipton tea, and cans, like Cadbury chocolate."

"It's all changing," said Harry. "Now we're all wearing Broadway shirts from Hong Kong."

"The Chinese are now manufacturing a lot of the goods in Hong Kong, but European companies are involved in investing money in Hong Kong," said Ivor.

"I wonder how the Arabs did their trading," said Chandran. "They didn't bring guns. But they managed to convert a lot of people to Islam."

"Arabs were good at convincing people. Even today they are very good at trading. They know what to exchange things for. I think they mainly carried jewellery, diamonds, and gems. It's all a bit difficult to imagine. But even today, there is a lot of trading done by Muslims," said Harry.

"Harry, what are your plans now that you are leaving college soon?" asked Chandran.

"Not sure," said Harry. "Might immigrate to Australia."

"Lucky fellow," replied Chandran "Take me with you."

They all laughed.

"I wish I could start a restaurant like Bake House or Green Cabin," said Ivor.

"Or Great Wall Chinese or Elephant house," added Ravin.

"Elephant House is very big company," Harry pointed out. " Old established families like the Gardiners and so on own these businesses."

"Where is the money?" asked Nada. "Which person would give money to one of us?"

"Nada's right. Stop dreaming," said Harry. "If you have a family business like Rex's Urban Stores on Main Street, you can think about these things."

"Harry's right," Chandran agreed. "Take Manik. His father owns F. X. Pereira. Or take Gulam Ali or Hirdramani. These are our classmates. But they have ready-made businesses. They are okay. Banks will take them seriously."

"As Tamils, we have more problems. You know what they say about Scotsmen; the road to London is their golden road. It's like that for us boys from Jaffna," said Ivor.

"Speaking of Tamils," said Harry, "did you hear that this Minister Cyril has said that he will get all the Tamils thrown out of Colombo?"

"Yes. I heard about it," Ivor told him. "Cyril has all the government trucks under his control. He wants to use the trucks to transport all the Tamils out and take over their properties. That's what I heard."

"It's because the Federal Party is asking for a Tamil province in the north and east," said Harry.

"Sinhala Only came first," Ravin pointed out. "Bandaranayake started it and became prime minister. The Tamils called for a federal constitution."

"True," replied Chandran, "but see what's happening; Cyril is getting all his thugs ready to burn all the Tamil businesses and houses."

"Why is it that most of the politicians behave like thugs?" Ravin wanted to know. "Take Cyril and his thug supporters. They are out of control and get support even from educated politicians."

"But you forget that we are the last of the English-educated fellows," Harry pointed out. "We sit in the same class and share the same jokes and laughs. But the juniors are all divided into Sinhala class and Tamil class. They never meet each other. They even feel hostile towards each other."

"That's right. The members of Parliament like Cyril can't even speak English. The only way for them to get noticed is to be violently anti-Tamil," said Chandran.

"I wish they'd pass a law saying that only graduates can enter Parliament." said Ravin.

"That won't save the Tamils," Ivor said. "Unfortunately, Tamils are the scapegoats for the failures of the governments. Even an all-graduate Parliament would not stop the troublemakers outside of Parliament. The problem is jobs. We have free education but no jobs."

"I guess you're right, Ivor," Harry conceded. "Educated youth down south are fed up with waiting for a better life. See how they live barely eating a square meal a day. Only the boys trained as carpenters and masons are getting jobs. Some are going overseas."

Two rings of the college bell signalled the end of lunchtime. The boys walked towards their classes.

***

Ravin cycled back home after school. It was a Friday, and the traffic was heavy. The cane basket that hung in the front of his bike, below the handlebar, carried his books and notebooks. The bicycle and the basket shook and rattled as he made his way along Darley Road to the junction at the Maradana Station, where Darley Road ended when it met the road running between Fort and Borella. A train went chugging past him below Darley Road, heading from Maradana Station to Fort Station, the final terminal for the trains running into Colombo.

The road coming from Borella became a bridge at Maradana. The railway platforms ran under the bridge, and the station was built above the platforms. It was a grand station well designed and boasting a clock tower a monument to colonial engineering.

If Ravin turned right, he would be heading towards Borella. He turned left and right soon after; passed Elphinstone Cinema, Buhari Hotel and its shops, and the Tower Cinema; and rode past Panchikawatte with its numerous car car parts shops. He also passed the road leading to Huftsdorp and the Supreme Courts. After passing St Anthony's Hardware Store and Mascon Hardware Stores, the timber shops; and bookshop where he sometimes bought books; and Capitol Theatre, he stopped at the crossroads. Trams, buses, cars, trucks, and bullock carts passed along coming from Grandpass and going to Pettah. The traffic policeman was hidden in the melee but could be seen by the cyclists as they weaved their way to the front of the traffic.

When the traffic policeman made a signal, Ravin and fellow cyclists were the first to get away, but they kept left, giving room to the cars and trucks, whose drivers tooted almost all the time to warn the cyclists. The traffic reached the roundabout, where more traffic came from the right, from Grandpass and Kelaniya, and headed into Pettah, with its markets, shops, and pavement hawkers.

Ravin waited for the traffic coming from the right, and when a small gap opened up, the car next to him moved forward and he surged along with it and they were clear of the roundabout. Ravin passed Pure Foods, a grinding mill that made rice, chilli and curry powder, and ground pepper and the place where Raman worked. He inhaled the spicy vapour wafting from the mill as he passed. This was Kotaboam Street, which ran for about two miles and ended at the harbour, meeting Mutwal Street. He cycled passed the two cinemas, Sellamahal and another; passed Modi & Co., which sold Walpamur water paint; and thought of Mr. Modi's lovely daughter, who visited his sister.

The Kotahena roundabout was approaching. Nice houses nestled on the right hand side, except for the furniture shop. Rows of smart houses could be seen set back from the road. He knew only the Pereras, who lived close to the roundabout.

There were vegetarian eating places close to the roundabout and some shops. Instead of turning right onto Kotahena Street and struggling to ride the bicycle up the steep road, he cycled forward, passing the Kotahena market and Ceylon Oxygen Company on the right and the houses on the left. Dr Chacko, their family doctor, lived in one of them, and the Modi family lived almost next door to him. These were large well-designed houses, some with rooms upstairs. He had been to some of these houses with his grandmother and mother when he was a small boy. He was now a big boy and never went out with his grandmother.

He passed the toddy tavern, where many drinkers wearing sarongs were seated on the pavement, some drinking from bottles and some from coconut shells. Toddy was dispensed into bottles, which had to be brought into the tavern by customers. Customers without bottles, like labourers dropping in after work, were served in coconut shells. Alongside the tavern were more respectable drinking places, where the toddy was served in glasses at a higher price. These public houses served food as well, and people wearing trousers dived into these toddy and arrack shops. Sarong-clad people preferred the cheaper place, the tavern. Ravin had gone into the tavern once or twice, along with a friend. He noted that the floor was quite wet, possibly to wash away all the toddy dripped onto the cemented floor by drinkers wearing sarongs and shorts.

After the toddy tavern, there was a row of small houses. One of the drinking places next to the tavern was owned by an Indian who lived in one of the houses in that row. This Indian spoke Sinhala like a Sinhalese and seemed to be very well off, even though he wore a sarong, indicating that he had no formal education. He was married and in his thirties. Ravin came to know that this man persuaded the father and mother of a fifteen-year-old girl to give him the green light to become the girl's lover, in exchange for paying their rent and other expenses. Ravin knew the father and mother. The father was a tailor with a sewing machine. He was always given the job of tailoring all the children's clothes. Ravin used to pass their tiny house they had two rooms in a house and see the pretty little girl grow. Ravin thought she was one of the prettiest girls he had ever seen. The family was poor, and the father or mother would drop in to see Ravin's mother, sometimes to borrow a few rupees, when the family really got desperate.

After the tavern and the row of houses, there was a tall brick warehouse and a narrow lane next to it, wide enough only for cycles and pedestrians. The lane was known as Jaam Mudukku. Ravin rode into the lane as it was a shortcut to his house on Pickerings road. The lane was between the tall warehouse to the right and a wall to the left the wall separating rows of houses, one row facing Kotaboam Street and the other facing Pickerings Road. Further up the road, going towards the harbour and after the rows of houses that were possibly built for harbour workers, one came to an open area, followed by public toilets. Ravin had, on occasion, visited the public toilet with his friends, when they wanted to relieve themselves. On one side stood a row of yellow-stained ceramic squatting pans with no doors but with a wall to cover the pan and the man using it. On the other side was a tiled wall for urinating on, with a drain to carry the urine away to the sewer system. There was a toilet for females next door, with a wall separating the two sets of toilets.

After going through the Jaam Mudukku Lane, where men sometimes lifted their sarongs and urinated against the walls, Ravin turned right and cycled to his house next door to Bobby Arnolda's compound. Lifting the bicycle up the three steps, he parked it leaning on the wall in the tiny veranda.

He noticed a gunny (jute) sack hidden in the bushes and banana trees near the house. The gunny sack looked like it contained bananas or yams, but in fact it was full of toddy bottles hidden in the bag by the illegal drinking place on the road. Ivor and Ravin had opened the gunny sack one day. They'd poured some toddy into two glasses and had seen flies floating in the bottle. But Ivor and he had swigged the white milky-looking liquid and felt groggy almost immediately.

The family was having a visitor. Uncle Siva, who usually stayed for some weeks before finishing his work in Colombo, was visiting. He talked about international happenings and how Indian leaders were talking about bringing telephones to the villages and so on. The small table that mother used was given over to Uncle Siva during his visits. Several of his books and manuscripts lay on the table. It was rumoured that Uncle Siva wanted to go to England and was preparing his papers. He had lived in India, studying architecture. His liberal views were seldom listened to. But he always had uncommon ideas. He read books on popular psychology.

Ravin remembered reading parts of one of his books. It was called Auto Suggestion. It was about the role of the imagination in life. If a plank was laid two or three feet above ground level, nobody would hesitate to walk on the plank. But if the same plank was laid connecting two adjoining tall buildings, only a few daring men would attempt to walk on it. The reason was that the imagination of human beings played a big role in life. The book suggested that many problems that bothered a person, even illnesses, could be made to go away simply by saying, "Every day, in every way, I'm getting better and better." The imagination would focus on the problem, and the problem would get solved. The will did not come into play. The power of the imagination was vastly superior to willpower. Ravin was fascinated by the book. For the fifties, this was a revolutionary idea.

He mentioned the idea to one of his friends, who was troubled by his mother and father splitting up. The father paid for his being a boarder in a house with a family and going to school. His friend found that repeating the mantra to himself, focussing on the idea of getting betterhelped him to get feel better. Ravin mentioned the book to Ivor and others and they all agreed it was a great book.

Uncle Siva visited important people who would help him in his work. He talked about civil servants and how so-and-so suggested how to get over a problem. Even his uncle, who was a doctor in Jaffna, talked about civil servants. It seemed that civil servants held the keys to getting things done. But Ravin's friends at school were impressed by well-dressed gentleman from the companies who drove their children to school. Some sat in the car, letting the driver do the driving. They wore ties and long-sleeved shirts. Some held a can of cigarettes. The can had a cutter built into the lid to open the can. Ravin knew how to cut the aluminium cover of the can of cigarettes using the cutter. Uncle Joti was a smoker. Smoking was a bad habit as far the family was concerned, just like drinking. Ravin had seen his father smoking once or twice. He coughed after each puff and soon put it out. Father's friend Uncle Vijay used to drink and smoke. He dropped in after drinks and recited some poetry he had composed. He was considered a nuisance because he smelled bad after liquor but tolerated for his poetry.

Seeing Ravin coming in, his mother said, "Go and ask Gopal to come. The kerosene cooker is giving trouble."

Ravin walked out to the road and turned right to enter Bobby Arnolda's compound. The Alsatian dog was unpredictable. It was not a ferocious dog but a temperamental one. Many times, it ignored Ravin. After all, the dog knew Ravin as a neighbour who came into the compound every now and then, mostly to collect a ball hit over the wall with the cricket bat. Other times, like this one, Ravin was coming to see Gopal or some other mechanic. Ravin walked gingerly passed the office and went past the lift, which lifted the cars up for servicing. Gopal's job was to service the cars when they were lifted up. He sprayed the bottom of the car with diesel or some similar liquid. Walking past the main house, Ravin entered the area where employees were housed in small houses. Ravin walked up to Gopal's place. The door was open. He walked up to the door. As he looked in, he could see Gopal seated on a stool, eating his dinner. It was a plate of rice with a fried green kankun. Kankun, which grew in abundance near water, was the cheapest vegetable in the market. Ravin felt sorry that he had seen the Spartan meal that Gopal ate. Ravin asked him to come to their house when he had finished eating, to fix the cooker.

When he got back to the house and was about to change clothes, he heard a car tooting from the road and some yelling. He realized that Godfrey, Sunil, and Peri had come over to pick him up to go to the cinema. Godfrey was at the wheel, and Sunil walked up to the house to ask him to come. Ravin asked Sunil to sit for five minutes till he had a quick wash. Ravin's mother came and spoke to Sunil while Ravin got ready. A few minutes later, the four boys were on their way to the Empire Cinema. The film was a war movie with Burt Lancaster and Montgomery Clift. After the movies, they pulled up at Bambalapitiya junction for hoppers and seeni sambal. After that, they decided to check Nada out, since his house was only a few minutes away. They pulled up, hoping the domestic would be standing out and he could be persuaded to wake up Nada. But the house was in darkness. They made a din on the metal dustbin, and when the lights went up, they took off in case Nada's father was enraged.

The next day, Nada asked Ravin about who had come to his house. Ravin explained that they'd wanted to get him out to go out for a drive to Galle Face but that Peri had made a noise and they'd taken off. When Nada confronted Peri, he denied all knowledge of the drum being thrown. Nada said his parents were sure it was us who'd made the noise. But he would keep us out of trouble.

While cycling to school, Ravin thought about his up coming trip to Jaffna to do his studies. Ravin wanted to meet Radhi, the girl who Siri had introduced to him before he went to Jaffna. After all, according to Siri, the girl's parents were Tamils. Siri had introduced her one day when Ravin and Siri had been standing around at Siri's gate. The two sisters were walking back after school. As the girls walked past the house, Siri had said, "Hello, girls, meet my classmate, Ravin." The girls had said "hello" but nothing more.

Ravin felt awkward about the whole idea of hanging about on Flower Terrace waiting for the girls to walk back after school. Once, he had summoned the courage to do it, and he'd sat on his bike at the end of Flower Terrace. But he'd spotted a Lanchester Saloon coming towards him, and he knew Radhi's father drove a Lanchester. He turned his bicycle around and faced the other direction to avoid being seen by the father. Sure enough, it was Radhi's father. He had come to pick the girls up and drop them off. Radhi sat next her father, and her sister sat in the back. Ravin could see Radhi looking at him as the car drove past.

The next week, he repeated the effort and was rewarded by a long chat all the way from Flower Terrace to Alfred House Gardens. She was a pretty girl; her smile was fetching and her pony tail very charming. But she was four years younger, and this made him feel awkward.

He decided to leave school at two o'clock and sneak off without telling anyone. If he told Siri, Siri would mention his interest in Radhi to Nada and the others, and they would have a good laugh, and soon the whole class would get to know. Even the teachers might get to know. And then it could be something of a problem, even though the upper-sixth form was almost like a halfway house between university and college. The teachers never tried to treat you like a schoolboy. Nobody questioned your absence from school. It was each man to himself. If you wanted to study, you could study. The teachers were there, and you could talk to them.

Some boys were getting tuition. Some, like Kumar, were already in Aquinas University College doing courses for the London Advanced Level examinations taking a different route to a degree, a London degree. The Batchelor of Science in Economicscourse was considered highly desirable. So if you could afford it, why not go for it?

Ravin could not afford fees at Aquinas. One could be paying fees for four to six years depending on the course. At the University of Ceylon, the tuition was free. You only paid for your accommodation and food. Even that could be waived if you brought a letter from college or a parish priest or an official saying that your family could not afford to pay such fees.

As planned, Ravin left school after Mr. Kuruvilla's English class. He was late, but he could take a shortcut. He cycled past Union Place and took the Richard Pieris Ltd shortcut and was on Flower Road in ten minutes, in time to walk home with Radhi.

***

The school had a cricket match the following week. It was the big annual event between two Catholic Colleges St Joseph's and St Peters. While the grounds were being prepared for the match, Harry was mustering flags and rattles ready for the battle cries outside the cricket pitch. Before the match began, the pavilion was full of old boys, many with flags and loud speakers. Some sounded the worse for arrack, although it was only ten in the morning. The grounds looked a glorious green and immaculate. There was tension in the air as the Josephian captain and the Peterite captain came out to toss the coin.

St. Joseph's were batting first, and all felt the tension as the first ball of the day was bowled. It was a fast ball tossed to land close to the crease and rise to touch the bails. A stout defensive bat was shown to the ball, and it fell forward, rolling towards the bowler. The second ball was a repeat of the first, once again played defensively. The third ball seemed to be an off-spinner, pitching to the right of the batsman and heading for the wicket. The bat swung at the ball, and it flew over the fielder and was rolling towards the ropes. A quick two runs were made, and it seemed that a quiet start had been made. A resounding crack was heard as the next ball flew towards the wicket. It was a six, and there was a huge cheer from the crowd and the bugles blew and Harry ran out of the crowd, waving the college flag and dancing a jig.

By the end of the fourth over, the scoreboard showed twenty runs. The crowd stirred, as new arrivals were looking for seats next to friends. Then the bowler bowled a full toss and the batsman swung the ball to the left. The ball flew up and there was a gasp as it descended into the hands a Peterite fieldsman. The opening batsmen had made a reasonable start, and the next batsman faced the ball. The next ball fell very short and rose up flying towards the batsman's head. He ducked, and the ball rested in the wicketkeepers hands. The last two balls were gently tapped to safe corners and two runs added to the score.

The seventh over saw the fifty come up on the scoreboard, and there was clapping and the blowing of car horns and bugles. Harry danced the baila and was joined by his classmates and some old boys of the school. The baila songs caught on, and drums started beating around the grounds. A pair of spoons came out of somebody's pocket and provided a metallic beat. Two wickets fell to balls spinning like they were humming tops. By twelve and lunchtime, the score had passed the magic hundred runs.

Ravin was standing close to Harry when the umpire signalled lunch, after consulting the captains.

"Get this flag. We are going for a round," said Harry.

Ravin carried the large flag mounted on a two-metre long pole, and they walked to a truck. Lots of boys were already on the truck, all carrying rattles or drums or mouth organs. Some were dressed in fancy multicoloured shirts, and some wore clowns hats and fancy dress. The truck full of boys drove out of the gate quietly and drove along Darley Road towards Union Place. The drums began to beat, and the party songs started off. "Hai Hooi, babiachige bicycle eka" was sung with great gusto and as loudly as possible by the time they reached the end of Darley Road and turned left towards the town hall and the eye hospital. The pedestrians stopped and stared at the truck full of noisy boys. Some smiled and waved; maybe they were cricket fans and knew what was going on. The baila dancing shook the truck. The truck turned right and passed Rosmead Place, the town hall and Victoria Park and turned into St. Bridget's Convent. The gate was open, and the drumming got louder with voice levels raised to the maximum. The song had changed to "Inky Pinky Parlez Vouz".

One or two nuns peeked from various corners but kept their cool. Some girls came out with their teachers, possibly going to the grounds for netball, and a hoot rang out and whistles erupted. The girls giggled and pretended not to be amused. There were catcalls from the truck – "Mehe enna ko" (can you come here?). The truck drove along the school's main drive.

Some voices were saying, "Don't go inside, Harry." And Harry was shouting to the driver not to go inside the convent premises. There were boys who could be recognized by the teachers and reported to college and Fr Peter Pillai never failed to mention this at the first school assembly after the cricket match. Harry spoke to the driver, and the truck drove out.

There had been incidents in previous years, involving some boys who'd jumped out of the truck and squeezed some girls who were passing along. They'd somehow been spotted and reported on. They had been dismissed from school. This truckload of boys was being kept under control.

The truck came out of the school, turned left, and moved along the road. Some girls were walking along, prompting catcalls and whistles from the truck. The truck moved along Green Path and past the art gallery, heading towards Colpetty. The singing was in full swing again as the truck drove into the well known girls school, Ladies College. Lots of girls were out of the classes, and some of the boys called, "Hello", and, "Hello, darling". One of the boys in the truck was squatting and trying to hide under a flag. Ravin knew at least two girls in the school but did not think they would see him. Some girls were bold and stood their ground, saying "hello" in return and watching the baila dancing on the truck with big smiles on their faces. And then Harry spoke to the driver, and the truck headed out of the college. The diversion in the school was mild, and the boys were out before the authorities could be summoned.

The truck drove along Galle Road, causing a disturbance and halting traffic in places as drivers stopped to get a good look at the truck full of flag-waving and baila-dancing lads. When the truck reached St Bridget's Convent, the gates were firmly closed. Obviously, phone calls had been made, giving warning of the possibility of a truck arriving.

The boys returned along Thurston Road and Bullers Road, turned left at Independence Square, and were back at Union Place, heading back to college. The voices of the singers were getting hoarse after an hour of loud singing. The crack of the bat hitting the ball could be heard, and all went quiet to avoid being spotted by the school authorities.

Harry and the boys returned to the cricket grounds and took up strategic positions in the pavilion. The score had passed the century mark, and there was an expectation of an excellent, unsurpassable score as the batsmen were driving the ball firmly and willing to run. Harry galvanized renewed energy, and the rattles whirred and the rubber car horns blared as each ball was hit. The noise and the entertainment made sense to Ravin as the interval between the batsmen getting the runs and the balls being bowled was better spent being entertained.

Ivor met up with Ravin, and they talked while they watched the match.

"What happened? You were nowhere to be seen when we went out in the lorry," asked Ravin.

"I was being briefed by my brother. Because he is in the Army, he gets to know these things. The situation is not good. Minister Cyril is preparing for a big hit on Wellawatte because a lot of Tamils live here. We live in Wellawatte, and we must be prepared, he said. There will be a lot of thugs who will be brought in, and they will be told which houses belong to the Tamils. The police are also roped into this. The Sinhala Buddhists in the police forces have been told not to intervene. So there will be no help coming from the police," Ivor told him. "The army might have to step in to stop the damage."

"What about the rest of the country?" Ravin asked. "Tamils live upcountry, in Kandy and Hatton. How about them?"

"At this stage, tea plantation Tamils from India are all right. They have kept quiet. They live in traditional Sinhalese areas. They will never ask for anything because they came from India to work in the plantations. They mostly live on plantations, and they can go back to India," said Ivor.

"I guess Colombo is the target. But you know, we have always lived in Kotahena. I have lived in Kotahena since my birth. I've lived on the same road for the last eighteen years. We know everyone. The thugs down the road know us. They are all Sinhalese, but the fights are among themselves," said Ravin.

There was loud clapping, and the boys stopped talking. The first of only six runs for the day was scored. The car horns blared and rattles rattled, and Harry and some boys danced the baila on the edge of the grounds.

"Don't be fooled by this," warned Ivor. "The thugs down the road may not attack you, but it's the thugs being brought in from outside who will attack you and the family. You must be prepared."

"But we know all the Sinhalese living on the road," Ravin protested. "We can ask for help from our Sinhalese neighbours."

"Don't be sure they will help," Ivor replied. How can they help? Are they going to come to your house and stand guard at your door?"

"I guess we could go to their houses and they could hide us," Ravin suggested. "But that means the thugs can loot the house."

"This is part of the plan. If the Tamils living in the house don't come out, the houses will be burned. If the people in the house come out, the houses will be ransacked," said Ivor.

"So they want the things in the houses," said Ravin.

"Yes. The minister has support from Buddhist monks and a lot of Sinhalese people who think the Tamils are holding good jobs and own too many things. They want to get the things out first and then burn the houses," Ivor explained.

There was shouting and some noise around the grounds as the batsman was given out leg before wicket. The last pair of batsmen was now on the pitch, and the score had reached 170. The mood of jollity remained on the Josephian side of the pavilion. The bullto seller was walking past. Ravin and Ivor bought bulltos and sucked on the sweet and sour, dark brown, home-made toffee.

"Still I am a bit doubtful," said Ravin. "The government won't let this happen. The police who walk down the road every day know us. We can run to the police station and bring the police."

"You don't understand," Ivor told him. "It's the government that is really behind it all. The prime minister is letting Minister Cyril do the dirty work. You think the cabinet doesn't know about what's going to happen? They jolly well know. But they want to let it happen."

The day after the passing of the Sinhala Only Act, the streets looked the same. But some people refused to pay their bus fares, saying that the government, which owned the buses, belonged to the people and, therefore, should not be asking for bus fare.

CHAPTER SIX
EXAMINATIONS

Examinations were approaching, and Ravin decided that he has to concentrate on his studies. He told his parents that he would like to go to Nuwara Eliya and stay with his Uncle Bala and Aunty Padma and do his work undisturbed by distractions.

Letters were written. The postal service was very good. Letters arrived within a day or two and got delivered to the house. Telegrams were faster. They were delivered at the address within one or two hours.

His train ride to Nuwara Eliya was pleasant. The train slowed down a lot at the sharp climb at Kadugannawa. One could walk along the train as it struggled to pull the load up the steep climb. People sat at the open door and dangled their feet. Looking down, only two or three feet away from the track, was a long drop along the cliff side to the bottom, maybe two hundred feet below.

The train pulled up at Peradeniya. The ride from Peradeniya was very pleasant, as the air was clear and cool, disturbed only by the hoot of the train and the tiny bits of coal dust flying out of the engine. The people were all very quiet, not talking, simply waiting to reach their stations.

Ravin was met at the station by his uncle and was in his cosy room with a heater in a few minutes. After dinner, he got inside his sheets and started reading the books and notes he had brought.

The notes he had made came in very handy, as he could write short notes and go over the notes to remember the subject. He read some poetry and tried to remember some. One of his subjects was English, and he was sure that some of the questions would be on Donne, T. S. Eliot, and Powys. Enjoying the sentiments expressed was one thing but remembering the lines was another. How does one write about Donne and say, "The poet expresses his love for his lover in the poem", without quoting the words?

Government was much easier. Comparing and contrasting unitary and federal constitutions was a piece of cake. But little did he realize that democracy – "government of the people, for the people, and by the people" – could easily become "government of the majority, for the majority, and by the majority". The problem had set in. Places at the university could be allocated according to the population distribution 75 per cent for the Sinhalese; 20 per cent for the second largest group, the Tamils; and 5 per cent for the rest. Ravin noticed that members of selection boards of government organisations were mostly from the majority community. He felt that these members of selection boards will discriminate in favour of the majority community. The laws were changed to make Sinhala the language of government administration. Tamils and other minorities had to become proficient in Sinhala in order to hold a government job. Even government offices in the north were conducting business in Sinhala. All government forms were only available in Sinhala.

The young aspiring students in the north and east were already protesting, and parliamentarians representing them were vigorously protesting. Some were even threatening to form a separate state.

In the mornings, after breakfast, Ravin worked for two or three hours and then went for a walk. He'd wear a jumper. It was cool even at midday. He went to the park and walked among the flower gardens, enjoying the vigorous bracing air. Many men wore woollen caps, shirts, and jackets but sarongs below the waist. Women wore saris and cardigans. Some wore a cloth tied at the waist like a sarong and a short blouse. Not many wore shoes. Most wore slippers. Some wore socks and sandals.

The hotels looked very impressive, especially the Grand Hotel. He walked into the lobby and looked around but was too intimidated by the luxury and finery displayed. What if a waiter approached him and offered him refreshments? "Can I help you, sir?" Just too embarrassing when he only had a few rupees in his pocket enough to buy a cup of tea in a little tea place.

He returned to the house by lunchtime and had a hot rice and curry lunch with lentils and fresh vegetables, which grew in profusion on every hill not growing tea. There were carrots, beetroot, cabbages of different colours, potatoes, aubergines, ladies fingers, yams of different sizes and shapes, capsicums, tomatoes, beans, pumpkins, cucumber, and lots more. Local fruit was in plenty too.

Thanks to the cool climate, Ravin never felt like sleeping even after a large lunch. His uncle came for lunch but was off soon after. Being a gynaecologist, he was always in heavy demand. Aunty was cooperative as always, never grumbling even if he had to rush off at night.

By being away from Colombo, Ravin was able to make a lot of progress with his studies. His stay of two weeks was very useful, but he was missing home.

CHAPTER SEVEN
THE BULLIES

R avin returned to Colombo after two weeks. It was a Saturday afternoon. The newspapers had run stories on the happenings in front of the Parliament. Tamil members of Parliament had staged a silent protest, a satyagraha, like Mahatma Gandhi had done in the days of the British Raj. There had been reports of possible attacks by thugs, and Ivor had warned of the possibility. But Ravin did not suspect anything would, in fact, happen.

In the morning, Ravin felt that there was enough activity on the roads to venture out. He walked out to the road and walked towards the harbour. This part of the road was very quiet for an early Saturday morning. As he reached the top of the road, the last shop was a Jaffna Tamil man's shop, Ponniah Store. It was a Jaffna cigar store, selling the dark hand-rolled Jaffna suruttu (cheroots). The shop had been burned down.

A chill ran down Ravin's spine. This shop had been always there, all eighteen years of his life. Fear gripped him. Who could have done this? How was Tamil leaders asking for a federal constitution related to burning down a long-standing store? Were the men walking on the street responsible for this?

It was true that most of the men walking on the street were uneducated – the labourers. But they were Buddhists, following "the Noble eightfold Path" of doing no harm to others, being kind to even animals, and not killing animals for food. Maybe one more principle had been added in Sri Lanka, Ravin thought if people were non-Buddhists, the eightfold path need not be applied to them; you could burn them and their property. You could just do whatever you wanted to do because the people you were harming were non-Buddhists.

Ravin wondered what had happened to Ponniah and his family. They ran the store as a cigar store, but they had stationery items and similar items at the back of the store. This was the only Tamil-owned store at this end of the street.

Ravin immediately felt scared. If such a terrible thing had happened, he could be accosted on the street and assaulted or even worse. Fear gripped him. He did not know what he should do now. Could he walk back home on this street? He knew every person who lived on this street. Should he walk along the other road and come back to Pickerings Road through the little lane connecting the two roads? The eating place next to Ponniah's shop was owned by a Sinhalese man. Next to the eating place was the entrance to a large number of small houses set at the back of the street where harbour workers lived. After that, there was a grocery store run by a Sinhalese man. Ravin's father had an account here, and the family did a lot of shopping here, buying vegetables, rice, flour, and sugar. Ravin wanted to ask questions of the people walking on the street.

"What happened to Ponniah's shop?"

"Who burned Ponniah's shop?"

"Why did they burn Ponniah's shop?"

"Where are Ponniah and the family?"

But he felt scared to even stop any of the men who lived down the road. They were all Sinhalese men. They could easily turn nasty.

Opposite Ponniah's shop was the back end of the Foreshore Police Station. It was a large station with a large set of houses and barracks inside the brick walls and a large playground that was used by the public for football and cricket. The police in the station should have noticed that there was a fire. There was no sign that the fire engine had come. The fire engines were parked not very far from the police station. Fire services were manned mainly by Malay men who would not misbehave.

Ravin walked along the road back home, feeling as if he was being watched by the street men. Suddenly, he did not belong to the street anymore. He was not a part of this community of Sinhalese, Tamils, Burghers, and Muslims who lived down the road. He was a Tamil boy, a vulnerable boy, among Sinhalese thugs. Usually the thugs fought among themselves.

Ruben Singho was a thug who'd managed to improve his life. He ran an eating shop and an unlicensed drinking place. He was the local thugs leader. He could have plans to burn Tamil shops and take them over. Only the police stood between him and complete control of all the Tamil shops in the street. But here was proof that the police would not intervene.

Ravin felt safer as he got closer to home. He passed Arnolda's garage and entered the compound where he lived. And then he decided to check if anything had happened to the store run by the Kerala Indian man. He walked back to the street and turned left. The Sinhalese man's store was open. But the Kerala man's store was closed, and the shutters looked different. Getting closer to the store, Ravin could see that the shutters were blackened and that the store had been broken into and set on fire. The street boys were walking along, not showing any emotion on their faces.

He stopped at the Sinhalese man's store and bought some biscuits.

"What happened to that store?" he asked in Sinhalese.

"Some boys burned it," the man replied. "These Indians should not be running shops here." he added. He was a very dark swarthy man from the deep south. He looked like an African. His eyes were large and piercing, and his hair was short and curly.

Ravin shook his head as if he agreed with the sentiment and walked back towards his house. It was obvious that the man had had a hand in the burning of the Kerala Indian man's shop. His eyes burned with the pleasure of having eliminated competition.

Ravin's head felt dizzy. He did not know what he should say to his family. Should he make them feel the fear that gripped him by telling them the truth? Should he pretend that all was normal and go about the day as if there was nothing unusual going on? After all, the family need not panic, since the event had happened and maybe was now under control by the police. In the end, he decided to tell his mother that the shops had been burned down.

"Something has happened to Ponniah's shop," he told his mother.

"What's happened?" she asked.

"It looks like there was a fire. Maybe the thugs set fire to the shop. It's burnt down. Even the Malayalee shop near the cooperative store has been burned," he said.

"You have to be careful," his mother warned. "Just because you speak Sinhalese well doesn't mean you are safe. Don't go too far."

"I won't go too far. But I need to go to the library," he replied.

Ravin's mother did not respond.

Ravin went to the library in the morning. He did not see any shops burned down in Pettah or Fort. He dropped in at Siri's house in the afternoon.

"Some shops were burned down on our road," Ravin told Siri.

"These thugs are trying to loot the goods. They clean out the shop when the shopkeepers run away," said Siri.

"You are right. There was nothing left in the stores," said Ravin.

"You must be careful," Siri told him. "They are stopping buses and asking people to speak in Sinhalese. If they don't speak in Sinhalese, they get a beating. But you can speak Sinhalese. You have nothing to worry about. Still, best to avoid going in buses."

"Being a Tamil has become a very big problem now," said Ravin. "I don't feel safe in Colombo anymore."

"Don't worry. This will stop soon," Siri assured him. "After all, a federal constitution is nothing big. It's a small matter. It's the politicians who are trying to use this to fight the elections. The thugs get a chance to make some money."

Siri's reassurance did not make Ravin feel much better.

They decided to visit Nada and cycled up to De Fonseca Road. The three of them rode out to the Saraswathi Lodge.

"Looks like your areas are not too bad compared to Kotahena," said Ravin.

"Most shop owners on Galle Road are Sinhalese. It's the houses that could be attacked in these areas," said Nada. "The badly hit areas are Ratmalana and Mt Lavinia."

"Why can't the government stop this?"asked Ravin.

"The government won't do anything because they want to teach the Tamils a lesson. My uncle said the politicians and their thugs are well organised. Minister Cyril has the electoral list and has identified Tamil houses on every street." said Nada.

"But what about the police? It's their job to protect people," said Ravin.

"Police are not interested. Why should they risk being on the wrong side of the politician's mobs?" said Siri.

"Why not call the army?" asked Ravin.

"That's where you are wrong," Nada told him. "Only the prime minister can call out the army in peacetime. It's not going to happen because he wants to teach the Tamils a lesson for making all these protest meetings in the north. My uncle said that the prime minister is refusing to do anything to stop the thuggery. He was seen in the Sinhalese Sports Club drinking whisky and refusing to discuss the matter. The governor general wants to stop the thugs."

"True," agreed Siri. "It's not safe for you be on the road, Ravin," he warned. "You better get back. Bambalapitiya and Colpetty areas are okay. We are okay. But you must get home."

There was nothing unusual going on the roads when Ravin cycled back home. Pickerings Road seemed unusually quiet, with only a few people walking on the road.

When he got home, he changed into his sarong. He sat on a chair in the sitting room with a book and looked out to the road. It was getting dark, and he got up to switch the light on. He saw men running on the road. This meant something unusual was happening something like an argument or a fight. Then it occurred to Ravin that Nada and Siri had warned him that there could be attacks on Tamils. So he walked up to the door. Ravin's mother must have noticed activity on the road from the bedroom window. She came to the front door and stood next to Ravin.

"Don't go out now," she said, and added, "There were rumours that the thugs were going to attack Tamil houses."

The shops and houses that they could see had closed their doors. Only thugs were seen running in large groups. Neither Ravin nor his mother had seen these men before. There were no police to be seen.

A large number of thugs gathered at the top of the compound. They were looking at Ravin's house. Some had long knives with them. Some held firebrands, and some held sticks and batons. It looked like they were getting ready to come into the compound of five houses, and Ravin's was the first they'd reach. Fear gripped everyone. They closed the door and bolted it. The upper part of the door had glass windows, and the family gathered at the front door. Ravin's sister was almost crying.

Ravin's mother said, "Son, go to the back door and talk to the Pereras. Ask them if we can go there."

The Perera family was Sinhalese, but they had a Tamil boarder staying with them.

Ravin slipped out through the back door and walked through the back garden full of banana trees and entered the Pereras' back garden. The house had no fencing. Ravin walked towards the back door. It was shut. After hesitating a moment, he knocked on the door.

"Who is it?" asked Mr Perera in Sinhalese.

"Ravin, Ivan's friend," said Ravin. Ivan was Mr Perera's son.

Mr Perera opened the door slightly and asked, "What do you want?"

"Mother asked if we could come over to your house because a lot of thugs are standing at the entrance to our compound with knives and firebrands. If they come to our house and set fire to it, can we come to your house?" asked Ravin.

"You can't come to our house," Mr Perera replied. "If those thugs found out, our house could be attacked."

Ravin's heart started beating. The Pereras' house was the only house without a fence and the easiest place they could escape to. The other neighbours without a fence were inside the same garden compound, but they were also Tamils from Pondicherry, and there was no hope that the thugs would not set fire to the houses they lived in.

Suddenly the mob moved away towards the shops, towards the junction of Pickerings Road and Santiago Street. Ravin's family stood watching the street until late at night. One by one, they went to bed. Ravin and his father stood at the front door till very late. There was running on the road. But the mob seemed to have gone elsewhere.

The next day, the family washed and dressed as usual. Ravin's sisters were in their white Good Shepherd Convent uniforms. But the big question was was it all right to go out on the street? Usually the two girls went out first and Mother left a few minutes later. Ravin's father had already left for work. He seemed to be unfazed by the dangerous activities during the nights. It was the third day after the attacks on the Tamils had begun. Maybe the thuggery had stopped.

Ravin got ready to go to the college. He left a bit early to cycle around a bit before going to college. He thought he would go up Santiago Street, cycle up towards College Street, and then turn right and head for Kotahena Street, where he would go downhill and turn left and head for the college. He cycled up Santiago Street. There were no Tamil-run shops on Santiago Street except the one that had already been burned down. He knew that the Emmanuels lived on the corner of Santiago Street and Wall Street. They were Tamils from Jaffna. As he passed the back of their house, he decided he would cycle around the area in the evening. He was going to be late for college.

In the college, the talk was all about the happenings in Ratmalana and Mt Lavinia. Tamils living in Mt Lavinia had been attacked. Some people had died in their houses because they'd refused to come out when the thugs had asked them to before setting fire to the houses. Many Tamil people were now homeless and had come to the temples in Wellawatte and Bambalapitiya to stay in a safe place.

"What makes you think the thugs won't attack the temples?" asked Chandran.

"It could happen I guess," replied Ravin. "But where can they go?"

"The thugs are mainly Buddhists. They won't attack temples," said Harry.

"In Wellawatte, the thugs went into houses and chased the Tamils out. They knew Tamil houses and only attacked them. They carried away everything inside the houses jewellery, brassware, anything that was of some value. Some friends of ours were so scared that their daughters would be raped that they gave everything away clothes, shoes, and household things," said Ivor.

"We were lucky I guess," Ravin told his friends. "How did it happen? Did the thugs break the doors? We shut our doors."

"The thugs banged on the doors. There was a large group near the door. The leader was directing the group. He must be the man who had the papers from the Electoral Commission giving the names of the occupants," Ivor explained. "When Mr Ramanathan opened the door, the man at the door asked him, 'Are you Tamils?'. Mr Ramanathan replied, 'Yes.' 'You must come out of the house now,' the man told him. 'We are going to set fire to the house.'

"Mr. Ramanathan pleaded with the man in Sinhalese, 'Please don't do this. We have nowhere to go. We have no house in Jaffna or anywhere else. We are Colombo Tamils. I went to school in Colombo.'

"The reply was, 'We have our orders. You must come out. We won't harm you and your family. If you don't come out, you could be burnt.'

"Mr Ramanathan was really scared because he had two daughters, both teenagers. But the family stepped out and the thugs went in. All the valuables were taken from the bedrooms and quick searches of the cupboards were made and anything attractive quickly removed. Then they threw some kerosene into the house and set fire to the house and walked away."

"This is like what happened to the Emmanuels in Kotahena," said Ravin. " The thugs didn't even wait for the people to come out. Apparently, the thugs were local ones. Even women were coming in and taking things away. They cleaned out everything they could carry, even the mattresses."

"This is a bit like when the bus services were nationalised," commented Chandran. "Do you guys remember? Many people refused to pay fares, saying that the buses belonged to them. Why should they pay? 'Ape Anduwa,' they said. 'This is our government. Why should we pay? Things in your houses belong to us. So we are taking them.'"

"Talking of buses, I couldn't have come by bus," said Ivor. His eyes showed fear. His voice was strained. "The politician's thugswere asking Tamils questions in Sinhalese. Those who didn't answer back in the right accent were hammered."

Nada held Ivor's gaze for a moment. He turned towards the sea as if he was trying to figure out something. "My father said that a sugar plantation in Valaichenai was attacked by a fleet of government vehicles full of thugs with bush knives and machetes. When the Tamil workers ran into the sugar plantation, it was set on fire. Those who ran out were beheaded and hacked to death," said Nada. His voice sounded deep and he bit his finger nails nervously.

"We have to thank our lucky stars that we are in Colombo," said Peri. Ravin could sense the feeling of fear in Peri as he was attacked once at his home.

"Why is the government letting this happen?" asked Ravin.

"You know Kumar's uncle is the minister of finance. Stanley said that the prime minister is refusing to do anything. Now only the governor general can call for an emergency and get the army out on the streets. This is because the queen still has a place in the constitution. She will have to be told, I guess, because Sir Oliver represents the queen," said Ivor.

"I suppose the prime minister will be admitting that he is guilty of starting all this if he calls the troops out," said Peri.

"You know we are reading about the Colebrooke-Cameron reforms right now in class," said Chandran. "It's part of the syllabus for the examination on government. These two idiots were so stupid that they set up one system of government for the south, north, and Kandy. It was the blind leading the blind. Kandyan culture and laws are very unique, and so are the laws and customs in the North. The British officials, including the governor, opposed the proposal. But it got approved in the British Foreign Office. They messed it all up." Chandran was knowledgeable in such matters because his father was the chief magistrate of Colombo.

"I suppose we have to the blame the British for the mess we are in. The constitution drawn up by Sir Ivor Jennings did not do anything to put matters right," said Ravin.

"Yes. It all began in 1830 or round about that time. The Colebrook-Cameron reforms were hailed as a great leap forward. But it was really a leap in the dark and into the abyss. Look at the big mess we are in," said Ivor.

"We have politicians who are manipulating the people," he added. "We know Bandaranayake started it all by passing the Sinhala Only Act. This was political manipulation, but he was agreeable to a federal solution for the Tamils. Now we have another set of manipulators exploiting the baser instincts of the uneducated Sinhalese masses. They are telling the masses to forget the Tamils and their demands."

"We have to pray that a better breed of politicians will come to power then," said Ravin, holding his hands together.

They heard the bell ring and dispersed to their classes.

***

Ravin cycled back after school. At Maradana, he could see that one shop had closed. This could have been a Tamil man's shop. He used to drop in at a shop that sold curd with treacle. But he did not feel that he could do that now. He would be a Tamil person in a Sinhalese man's shop. What would they be thinking? Would they be laughing at him? Might they even chase him out?

Looking down Demotagoda Road, he dreaded thinking about what had gone on in Demotagoda. It was a suburb where lower middle-class and working-class people lived, and many working-class people were ruffians with no fixed accommodation. The Tamils were mainly middle-class people, clerks, teachers, engineers, doctors, lawyers, and health workers. The politicians, like Minister Cyril, were giving this as the reason for imposing a Sinhala-only language policy. By making Sinhalese the only official language, this imbalance would be corrected. The ruffians and thugs were mainly Sinhalese. In the Sinhalese villages, there was no such problem. All classes existed in the Sinhalese villages landowners, doctors, lawyers, teachers, nurses, native physicians, and uneducated rural poor persons eking out a living selling vegetables and providing labour for building houses and roads. In Dematagoda, a Colombo suburb, the situation was different. The professionals were mainly Tamils, and the labourers were mainly Sinhalese. The resentment was expressed in Parliament. When it came to voting, there were many more labourers and lower middle-class persons who could vote for a Sinhalese candidate. No Tamil could win a seat in Parliament in the south. He could be a famous lawyer, but when it came to voting, there was no possibility that he could win against a Sinhalese person, even a clerk or labourer.

The trade unions representing government workers were now openly advocating that only Sinhala Buddhists should be appointed to important positions in the government. The Sinhalese politicians had ensured that Sinhalese would be appointed to senior government positions by legislating for Sinhalese only as the official language. Promotions within the government depended on proficiency in Sinhalese. To apply for promotions or even to hold onto the job, one had to pass the Sinhalese language proficiency test. If you did not want to sit for the test, you could resign and be entitled to a small pension. Many Tamil government servants resigned. Even many Sinhalese and Burghers resigned on the language issue because they could not see a future for themselves in the government service. Many Tamils, Burghers, and Sinhala Christians thought they had no future in the country. These thoughts ran through Ravin's mind as he reached home.

He reached home, knowing that his mother and sisters and grandparents would be at home because they rarely travelled out. His mother and sisters went to the Good Shepherd's Convent, which was at the top of the road. His grandmother did her visits to neighbours only. Grandfather rarely walked out. He was not the visiting type. Once he was in the house and his father was in, everybody was at home.

"How was your day?" asked his mother. "Was there anything happening?"

"Nothing was happening. But I heard that the Tamils living in Mt Lavinia and Ratmalana were attacked," he replied.

"It was the night before," Ravin's mother told him. "Now the army has been called out. The teachers were talking about Ratmalana in school. Thambiah, one of the Queen's Counsel, was attacked. The thugs took away all the things in the house and set fire to it. Some of the thugs hid the stolen money under books they'd stolen in a drain not far from the house. The uncle of one of the teachers is the air force officer who was in charge of the area. He noticed books lying in the drain and took them out. There was a lot of money lying under the books. He put the books back to cover the money but not before noticing that the title of one of the books was The Rule of Law in Sri Lanka and that it was written by the same member of the Queen's Counsel who was attacked in his house. Apparently, the poor man was beaten badly and nearly died before they let go of him and the family took him away.

"This air force officer I think his name was Milroy de Soyza told his men to keep a lookout for the man who'd hidden the money under the books. The thief did not want to share the money with the other thugs. He'd hidden the money, and he was going to come back for it. One of the soldiers hid behind a tree and waited for the thug to return. He did return, and they caught him with his loot, red-handed. He got his beating before they took him to the police station with the money."

"In Mt Lavinia, it was the same thing," Ravin replied. "The thugs were led by important-looking people, maybe party workers or government officials from outstations, who knew which houses were occupied by Tamils. They beat some of the people, and all the things in the house were removed. They were as usual keeping their jewellery in the cupboards. The thugs asked for these items specifically, demanding, 'Where are you keeping the jewellery?' And then everything was taken. You have to call this daylight robbery, not a communal riot," he concluded.

Tamils keep their savings in jewellery. Mothers pass on their jewellery to their daughters.

"This is true," Ravin's mother agreed. "They came to rob and beat the Tamils. Apparently the prime minister had blamed the Tamils for starting the riots. He had given a talk over the radio saying that all this started because the mayor of Nuwara, Eliya, was killed by Tamil people.

"What a shame for the prime minister, an Oxford University educated man, to provoke the Sinhalese with this allegation. He was actually encouraging the Sinhalese to take revenge, wasn't he?" she asked.

"Yes," said Ravin. "Even the middle-class Sinhalese will encourage the hooligans to go about beating Tamils and stealing their property."

"The worst atrocities were in Polonnaruwa, son," she said, taking a deep breath. Her eyes closed for a moment. "the thugs killed more than 100 people there. These Tamil people were brought to work in the sugar cane farm. The Sinhalese thugs were transported by government vehicles to Polonnaruwa, and they chopped people to death. They chased out those who ran into the sugar cane plantation by setting fire to the sugar cane. When the people came out to escape the fire, they were chopped to death."

"Somebody said that 300,000 Tamils from Colombo have been moved to Jaffna by boat," Ravin added. "Must be Tamil people from Ratmalana, Moratuwa, and further south."

"It's a good thing that they're out of harm's way. You never know what these thugs will do. Even ministers are the same. They might set fire to temples full of Tamil refugees," she said.

"I feel very unsafe nowadays, Mother," said Ravin.

"Yes, son, I feel the same," she confessed. "But where can we go? Father and I work in Colombo. Finding teaching jobs in Jaffna won't be easy. And schooling is another problem. We are lucky that all three of you are going to good schools."

"Some people have gone overseas. It seems to be the best thing for us," Ravin suggested.

"But we don't have the money. That solution is all right for people who have the money," she replied.

"Maybe I will try to go first and send tickets for all of you when I get a job," said Ravin.

***

The next day, Ravin went to school. The class was doing government and the lesson was on the constitutions of countries. The class were studying the evolution of the Constitution of Sri Lanka. There were parallel developments in India. The various regional administrations were being reorganized in India. Similarly, in Sri Lanka, the Colebrooke-Cameron reforms brought about a unified administration, combining the north, the south and the Kandyan administrations.

After school, Siri asked Ravin to come home with him, and the two cycled together to Colpetty. They decided to stop at Bake House for tea and patties. After the tea, they decided to go to the beach.

Ravin and Siri were seated on the stones at the beach at Colpetty, having cycled along the Alfred House Gardens Road and crossed the Galle Road.

Ravin was hesitant to ask Siri an awkward question about how he felt about the federal solution. Siri was a Sinhalese Buddhist, and he may be embarrassed by the question. After thinking about the pros and cons of asking the question, Ravin blurted out, "Why do you think we are having this problem between Sinhalese and Tamils?"

"The problem came up because the Bandaranayake government declared Sinhalese as the official language for conducting government business," Siri responded, "and the Tamils, Muslims, and Burghers had to pass the language tests for promotions. The Burghers left as fast as they could. Tamils are also leaving."

"What made the government make Sinhala the official language?" asked Ravin.

"Because Bandaranayake wanted to be the prime minister. He was passed over for leadership by Prime Minister D. S. Senanayake, who wanted his son to take over. The only way to gain power was to wave the communal flag. This was a risky political gamble, in the sense that Tamils and other minorities would feel discriminated against. But it had to be done to win the elections," replied Siri.

"Do you think a devolved state, like a federal state, will be the answer?" asked Ravin.

"Why do Tamils want a federal state?" asked Siri.

"Because they feel discriminated against by the government," replied Ravin.

"In what way?" asked Siri.

"Take government jobs, for example," Ravin said, "It is very difficult for a Tamil to find a good job in government."

"Why not concentrate on the private sector?" asked Siri.

"Most companies are run by the Sinhalese. So in this climate, the best man may not win," replied Ravin.

"Tamils can go into business. Do you think the banks favour the Sinhalese?" asked the Siri.

"That's true in one sense. But the minority faces more difficulties," Ravin said. "But if you analyse it," he continued, "Tamils have a deep sense of fear fear of violence and bloodshed in the streets and homes."

"But it was the street thugs who carried out these acts of violence," said Siri. "Many Sinhalese helped the Tamils to survive" said Siri

"Yes. That is true," Ravin conceded. "But the fear remains. The police and the soldiers could not be depended upon. There is a sense of uncertainty. It's this fear that makes most Tamils leave Sri Lanka, if they can. It is not an imagined fear. There is a feeling of resentment among the Sinhalese, especially among the labouring classes."

"Maybe so," said Siri. "But this cannot be eliminated until we have a more equal society in Sri Lanka. That will take more time to resolve."

Ravin remained silent for a while before he said, "I think that, if we study the animal worlds, we can see that each group of animals, whether monkeys, lions, or dogs, has its own territory. I think this is very true of the human species too. Look at what happened to the Jews in Germany and other parts of Europe, after Jewish and German populations had lived together for hundreds of years. In the United Kingdom, after so many hundreds of years of living together, the Scots, the Irish, and the Welsh are still asking for independence. When England was playing France, the Scots cheered for the French. Human beings, like animals, are territorial. Tamils need a piece of territory to call their own. Somewhere to run to when the thugs go on the rampage"

"I see your point," said Siri. "But Sri Lanka is such a small country."

"Its population is almost as big as Australia's," Ravin replied. "Siri, what do you think about a federal solution?"

"The word federal is not acceptable to most Sinhalese. Some other word may be acceptable. But here the problem is the area of land being demanded by the Tamils," Siri said.

"What is an acceptable area for a devolved state?" asked Ravin.

"That is not easy to answer. The Tamils are demanding an area of land not in proportion to their population," said Siri.

"How do you think our problem will get sorted out?" asked Ravin.

"Tamils will not get a federal state, that's for sure," said Siri.

"I'm also convinced that the fact that the Sinhalese consider themselves to be Aryans has something to do with our problem," Ravin added. "The Buddhist monks strongly believe that the Sinhalese culture is an Aryan culture and should be defended."

"I believe that too. Sinhalese is an Aryan language, and our culture has its roots in Aryan culture," replied Siri.

"No doubt there are links to Aryan culture and race," Ravin said. "But one could say that about Dravidian culture too. Sanskrit has provided many words to Dravidian languages like Tamil, and Hinduism is strongly rooted in Aryan culture. But the real problem is that the Sinhalese feel superior to the Tamils in a racial sense. They call the Tamils pariahs a low form of human beings. That has always been deeply rooted in the Sinhalese."

"I suppose there is a sense of superiority felt by the Sinhalese," conceded Siri. "But many Tamils are marrying Sinhalese and vice versa. That is helping to make a change."

"Yes," said Ravin. "It is still a slow process. Only a charismatic leader can lead a change in the attitude."

Siri and Ravin talked about the resentment felt by the Buddhists about the Christians and Catholics getting good jobs in the private sector. The government could not do anything because these were private companies.

It was getting dark, and Ravin cycled out along Galle Road heading for Galle Face. This seemed a safer route than going through Union Place and Maradana, where a lot of thugs hung out.

When Ravin got home, his mother was standing at the door looking towards the road, as it had gotten quite dark. "Where did you go?" she asked. "You must get back home early. This is not the time to be visiting friends. Anything can happen."

"I was with Siri," Ravin told her. "We were taking a walk along the beach."

"Now that you are having term tests, it's best that you take your books and go to Jaffna. There won't be anybody to disturb you. You can stay in the upstairs room. Uncle Siva and Aunty Dhanaluxmi have moved into their new house. You can even stay in their new house," said his mother.

"All right," replied Ravin. "I will do that. I can get ready for the final exam. I can prepare short notes on all the topics."

Seated on the settee and reading the newspaper, Ravin's father was listening to the conversation. "Right now it's not a good idea to be travelling anywhere," he interjected. Things are a bit quiet, but the troublemakers are always waiting for a chance."

"I am saying that he can go in about three weeks when the schools close for the midterm break," Ravin's mother said.

"I might send some books when you are going to Jaffna. Appiah," he said, referring to Ravin's grandfather, "might be able to sell them at the bookstore."

"Don't make him carry a big suitcase. He has to take his own books," Ravin's mother said.

"Not too many books," replied Ravin's father. "Only about ten. Somebody will meet him at the Jaffna Station to carry the suitcase."

CHAPTER EIGHT
TIGER CUBS

The school holidays began, and Ravin was determined to catch up in all his subjects. Government was the easiest. The teachers gave plenty of notes on this subject. He especially liked comparing and contrasting the British Constitution with the Ceylon Constitution. That was easy. The Colebrooke-Cameron reforms and the Donoughmore Constitution, on the other hand, were very slippery and hard to remember.

Indian history meandered a lot, and so it was hard to get a grasp on. And the teachers of this subject didn't make it any easier. While Mr Rajapakse was pretty sharp and did follow the syllabus, the students had a lot of questions, so progress was slow. Mr De Silva simply read out loud from the book.

European history was excellent. There was plenty of action Louis the fourteenth building his palace when the people were poor and not able to appreciate his efforts, Napoleonic wars, the French Revolution, Richlieu, the Iron Chancellor in Germany, the Austrian Empire. But the Balkan problem was knotty, and Ravin could not formulate any clear thoughts on how to get a handle on that topic.

English was the toughest. The syllabus was broad, and it was difficult to write sensibly using simple words. Mr. Kuruvilla gave frequent exams that required sharp and pointed answers. Kuru circled long words needing a dictionary and inserted a simple word in it's place. Some students like Melville who liked long words were cheesed off with this. Plenty of quotations were required, which worried Ravin because this meant that he had to remember portions of poetry, writing, and drama. He enjoyed reading the texts but hardly ever remembered the exact word used. This was going to be difficult.

Uncle Thanga arrived from Jaffna with his wife on an urgent matter drugs and chemist supplies for his dispensary. There was a good chance that the drugs could be confiscated at Army or Police road blocks. So he had received a letter from the superintendent of Police to prove that he was medical doctor.

Ravin joined Uncle Thanga on the return trip. Ravin even got a chance to drive the Peugeot 203 on the long stretches of gravelly road on the A9 to Jaffna. Oncoming traffic worried him, but he was advised to ignore oncoming traffic and stick to his half of the road. This seemed to work well, and he gained a lot of confidence steering the car on long stretches.

Ravin, Uncle Thanga, and Aunty Punitham arrived in Jaffna feeling tired.

"You can stay at Navaler Kottam," said Uncle Thanga. "It's very quiet there compared to my place. Patients come all the time, and you will be disturbed. But come whenever you feel like it."

"You must come and visit us," added Aunty Punitham. "Our house is just a few minutes' walk away. Gopal will drive you to see some places when you are ready."

Ravin was warmly greeted by his grandparents and aunts. The travel bag was taken upstairs to the quiet room. He was given a towel, and he went to the well for a bath. The well water was refreshing. He was given tea and breakfast. And he went upstairs to catch up with his sleep. The place was very quiet, and the absence of radios blaring out popular songs from eating places was noticeable.

When he woke up, it was midday. He heard a crow cawing and a car go rattling by. He felt removed from the cacophony of Colombo. He was ready to study. He got his books out of his bag and assembled them on the table and got down to some work.

He heard his aunt asking the cook to go up and check whether Ravin was ready for lunch. Ravin walked down and had lunch. The country rice and fresh tasting vegetables whipped up his appetite. He sat with his grandmother and aunts and relatives and they chatted about his studies and the recent bad turn of events in Colombo. They mentioned that many families had come from Colombo, including the family of the government agent for Jaffna who lived in the large property behind Navalar Kottam.

Ravin returned to his room and resumed his studies. He had another nap and got up and resumed his studies. It was late afternoon, and he felt the urge to go out.

Ravin walked along the roads that he knew and reached Main Street. He walked along, looking at the shops. They were very quaint, very old buildings, and the items on sale were limited. There was no hustle or bustle. An air of contentment seemed to pervade the street. The place seemed like a vast monastery, where everyone moved slowly. The cyclists pedalled slowly, and the cars almost every car was an Austin Somerset seemed to move at the slowest possible speed to avoid stalling.

"Brother, are you from Colombo?" a voice called out breaking Ravin's reverie.

"Yes. My family and I live in Colombo," Ravin replied. "I came this morning."

Three young boys, maybe a little younger than Ravin, stood on the roadside. They were dressed differently and appeared to be Colombo boys.

"Were you having trouble in Colombo?" the young person asked.

"Not really. We live in Kotahena. There were many incidents, but we were not attacked. Are you living in Colombo?" asked Ravin, trying to confirm his impressions.

"I was living in Ratmalana," said one of the boys.

"I was living in Mt Lavinia," added the second one.

"We lived in Nugegoda. My name is Sri," said the third boy.

"To tell you the truth, I'm never going back to Colombo, even if my parents return to Colombo. We were all beaten up for nothing. Even when we were hiding in the school, they chased us and beat us," said Sri.

"What can you do here by yourself, without your parents?" asked Ravin.

"I'm going back only if I have a weapon," replied Sri. "Even a hand grenade will do. I will be hitting back at those no-good Sinhala thugs."

"You can't live your life waiting to take revenge," Ravin counselled. "You have to think of your future."

"It's all right for you," said Sri. "You never faced the Sinhala mobs."

"I do understand," Ravin told the boy. "We only narrowly escaped. The mob went to loot and set fire to the shops. So they got busy with some big looting and forgot about us."

"Call me Kuhan," said one of the other boys. "We are going to form a group of young fighters who will be waiting to respond to any thuggery in Colombo."

"You see already that the police are making trouble in Jaffna," said Sri. "They think they are the rulers of Ceylon. Some army men are also trying be the bosses of Jaffna."

"What do you mean, the Police are making trouble?" asked Ravin.

"Some young boys from Jaffna tried to argue with the Sinhalese shopkeepers here. It was unfortunate. The shopkeepers shut the shop and complained to the police. So the police and the army started bossing the place," Kuhan explained.

"The army is not the right thing for this problem," said Ravin. "They are not trained to handle law and order problems. They shoot first and ask questions later. That's how they are trained."

"We were forced to leave Colombo because of the Sinhala mobs terrorising us. Now we are facing the same problem here, our homeland," said Kuhan. "The only difference is that these thugs are wearing uniforms. Why should we put up with this? We are ready to fight, to die fighting."

"There are many young boys whose parents were killed and whose brothers and sisters murdered. These boys have formed a group to go to Vavuniya with guns from India," said one of the boys.

"That's right," Sri added. "We are second-class citizens in the Sinhala areas. Why should we be second-class citizens in the north too? No way are we going to let this happen. We are a group already. We meet at the school, at Central College. Twice a week we meet and discuss how we should build up resistance to the army. We have to get rid of the army."

"Why are they keeping the Army here?" asked Kuhan. "What's happening here to worry the boss men in Colombo?"

"I hope the emergency is lifted and the army is sent back," Ravin told the boys. "You see, everywhere, when you send the army to sort out problems, the situation gets worse. It's happening in Ireland. It happened in Vietnam. It's happening in Kashmere. It's happening all over Africa. I hope things cool down and the army goes back."

"Brother, if you want you can come to our meeting," said Sri.

"I'm here to do some studies," Ravin replied. "If I get some time, I will drop in."

"We meet at the Central College cricket grounds on Sundays around four in the afternoon," said Sri.

"Thanks for letting me know," said Ravin, and he and the boys parted company.

When Ravin got back to Navalar Kottam, it was getting dark. His uncles had dropped in to see him.

"I know you are here to study. Is everything all right in Colombo?" asked Uncle Anandan.

"Things are a little bit okay now," replied Ravin. "The army trucks drive along the road now and then, especially at night."

"We were worried, you know," said Uncle Siva. "A lot of people were killed by paramilitary thugs employed by some ministers. They used government vehicles to do their dirty work."

"There were some deaths even in Colombo," added Uncle Jothy. "Some families have come to Jaffna to escape the killings."

"Yes. I heard ships were used to send the people out of Colombo," said Ravin.

"Now already several groups of boys are meeting and planning to hit back at the politicians and their thugs. I can see their point. What is to stop those thugs from attacking us in the north? We don't have any weapons to defend ourselves," said Uncle Anandan.

"Yes. We are defenceless," agreed Uncle Siva. "Even the police are unreliable. Some Tamil policemen are here. But their bosses are Sinhalese. The army is completely useless for the Tamil man. It is the army manned and deployed by the Sinhalese. They will never defend us."

"The Sinhalese are worried that a federal state will be the beginning of some connection with Tamil Nadu and India," said Uncle Thillai. "The Buddhist priests want Ceylon to be a Buddhist country, and so they want to stop any federal solution. In the end, we have to live in this country. We have learned to make compromises. I personally think that our population is getting too big. There is land hunger. The government is trying to move the Sinhalese to the north because there is more land here. All these irrigation schemes are meant to cope with this expanding population."

"In a sense, we must learn to compromise," said Uncle Jothy. "The federal solution is the right one, but we are up against the Buddhist extremists. The young people in the south are looking for jobs that we used to do, like government jobs. What will be the compromise solution? I do not know.

"Anyway," he added, "you are here to study. We don't want to disturb your work. Why don't you have a bath or wash? The roads are pretty dusty."

"Yes," agreed Uncle Siva. "I must be going home. We will meet up later."

Ravin went upstairs to get his towel. After his wash, he had his dinner and did some reading before going to bed.

Late at night, he was woken up by the sound of a truck. The engine sounds were loud and came from a spot close by. He walked up to the window and looked out to the road. There was an army truck parked on the side of the road. Some army men were standing around, while two of them were dragging a young boy into the truck. Ravin realised that he was not safe on the streets of Jaffna anymore.

He could hear the sounds of people moving downstairs. He walked across to the staircase and saw that everyone had woken up. He got dressed and went downstairs.

He asked the cook, who was standing close to the staircase, about what was going on.

"They have Sekeran," the cook replied. "He went out to the shop I think."

"Who has him?" asked Ravin.

"The army," said the cook.

"Why do they want him? What's he done?" asked Ravin.

"He's done nothing. They are picking up young boys and taking them to the army camp," explained the cook. "This is happening now. Sometimes the boys never come back."

But the family knew the army had picked up Sekeran because Aunty Padma had looked out and seen Sekeran at a distance walking towards the house. She did not think there was any problem, but when he was about to cross the road towards the house, he was called towards the army van. He walked towards the van, and without any questions being asked, he was bundled into the van. She woke the people up, and grandfather opened the door. The truck took off as soon as the door opened.

The cook was sent to bring Uncle Siva and Uncle Anandan. They arrived quickly. The events were explained to them. They went off to wake up other relatives. One had a car and went to the police. The police took down an entry in the entry book.

"We can't go to the army camp at this time," said the police officer. "But we will go there in the morning. We don't have a truck anyway."

"Can you ring?" asked Uncle Siva. "We are very worried. You know about young boys being taken away and never being seen again."

"I'll ring now," said one of the policemen. He went to the phone and dialled a number.

The conversation was brief. He put the phone down.

"The army has no record of anybody being picked up. It must be a mistake, they said," the policeman reported.

"But my sister saw the boy being taken away," said Uncle Siva.

"Look, you know how it is in the army," said the policeman. "We can't do much. We can register your complaint and give it to the army people. If you know anybody in the army, you could try to find something out."

Uncle Siva contacted an army officer who was a Tamil and found out that all young boys who were picked up were sent to Boosa in the south. The boy's mother made daily attempts to meet various people and ask for help to find him. But there was no trace of him.

By the time Ravin left for Colombo, there was still no news of Sekeran. The army denied having picked him up.

Epilogue

Ravin woke up when he felt someone shake him roughly. He had been fast asleep in the Colombo Katunayake Airport and may have missed his flight maybe he was being woken up by the airline employees to rush him to the boarding lounge. He looked at his watch.

Several persons, some wearing uniforms, were standing next to him.

"Are you Ravin Cumaraswamy?" asked one person.

"Yes. Sorry I fell asleep. But there is another hour before boarding time," he said, getting up and reaching for his cabin travel bag.

"You have to come to our office first. We are airport security staff." said the swarthy person in uniform.

"But I'm going to be late. What is it that you want to know from me?" asked Ravin.

"We want to question you. We have orders to arrest you if you don't come now," said the man in uniform. The uniform was meant to look like a policeman's, but something was not right. The man himself did not look like a policeman.

"Okay. I'll come, but I need to get this flight because I don't have any more leave left," said Ravin.

"We will put you on the next flight out if you miss this flight," said the man in the uniform.

Ravin and the men walked towards the nearest door and exited the building on the tarmac. Ravin was surprised to see a white van parked right up next to the building. Only ambulances and emergency vehicles were allowed to come this close to the terminal.

Ravin's family members were frantic when he did not arrive on his scheduled flight. His wife and children returned home, and his wife rang Colombo. All she could find out was that Ravin had stayed with his friend on the last day of his visit and had left his friend's house for the airport. He had not contacted his friend since going to the airport.

Ravin's family contacted several prominent persons, including lawyers, executives, and persons with good political connections. But all their searches were in vain. There was no trace of his whereabouts. Ravin's family feared that Ravin may have joined the ranks of persons who had disappeared without a trace.